Was She Haunted by a Lover Who Lived 200 Years Ago?

She did not know. She only knew that she was possessed by the vision of this dashing, handsome 18th century man, whom she longed for with her heart and soul and all the stormy depths of passion that raged within her. . . .

SMOULDERING FIRES

She had lived and loved in another time . . . or had she?

Big Bestsellers from SIGNET

SMOULDERING FIRES

Anya Seton

A SIGNET BOOK
NEW AMERICAN LIBRARY
TIMES MIRROR

SIGNET TRADEMARK REG. U.S. PAT. OFF. AND FOREIGN COUNTRIES
REGISTERED TRADEMARK—MARCA REGISTRADA
HECHO EN CHICAGO, U.S.A.

SIGNET, SIGNET CLASSICS, MENTOR, PLUME AND MERIDIAN BOOKS
are published by The New American Library, Inc.,
1301 Avenue of the Americas, New York, New York 10019

FIRST SIGNET PRINTING, JANUARY, 1977

3 4 5 6 7 8 9

PRINTED IN THE UNITED STATES OF AMERICA

Foreword

This story germinated some time ago in one of those tiny intellectual curiosities about the identity of the actual Acadian woman behind Henry Wadsworth Longfellow's classic poem *Evangeline*. Having finished my novel *Green Darkness*, there was nothing more pressing on hand but some speeches, and the always welcome fan mail. I did some desultory reading on Longfellow's life in general, and on the Acadians in particular, thinking that no one seemed to have written any sort of *novel* about the Acadians and their exile. The seed sprouted one day when I was looking up some other historical fact in the Connecticut Colonial Records, and fell upon the startling entry quoted in this book. There were six of the exiled Acadians grudgingly accepted in Greenwich (my own home town) in 1756. That fact seems unknown to most people, but the entry suddenly dovetailed with my desire to write about a high school senior with an unusual problem, and then the whole concept burgeoned.

There ensued much research. Special trips to Nova Scotia and Quebec and a special trip to Louisiana—since I can never write about anything unless I've seen it. I live in Greenwich, and have done so at intervals all my life; I was therefore amused as well as dismayed to discover how little one really *sees* of one's own environment, until the seeing becomes deliberate. Focussed. I had to check mileages and geographical detail here, quite as carefully as I do in foreign locations.

This book also exhibits my considerable though lay interest in hypnosis and abnormal psychology. Moreover, I hope that it will serve to interest readers in a largely overlooked minority group—the French-speaking peoples of North America, but above all I hope that it makes a convincing, entertaining *story*.

All the characters are fictitious, all the places are real—except "Bellerive" on the Bayou Teche, which is a composite. The history throughout is as accurate as I can make it.

My fervent thanks to many kind people in Nova Scotia and Louisiana, who were enthusiastic about the project.

My thanks to the Greenwich High School, its teachers and many of its seniors, who patiently answered questions while permitting me to mingle among them and watch the school in action.

In the beginning I started to trace the "real" Evangeline, thinking that at least she might have been Emmeline LaBiche, as they think at St. Martinville in Louisiana. The Nova Scotian archivist flatly squashed that notion. He said that there was no Emmeline LaBiche at Grand Pré, and gave documentation. So I have presented a version of what *might* have happened to one anguished Acadian girl who was forcibly torn from her lover on the eve of marriage. And I trust that the "Smouldering Fires" of the title will be clear as referring to the buried fires, both actual and emotional in Amy's unconscious.

Chapter One

After the initial September day of confusion, Greenwich High School with its twenty-five hundred students was settling down, and Amy Delatour already felt herself as lost and lonely as she had been during her last two academic years here. She was now a senior, although only sixteen, and knew that her previous work—mostly straight As—had aroused a flicker of interest among the teachers, but she had no special friends, she belonged to no group or club.

During a free period in the Student Center Amy avoided all the activities around her and settled in a corner with a book, looking grim and unapproachable, dreading the year ahead, but realizing that, at least, the use of her brain gave some satisfaction. There was scant satisfaction at home, except when she could be alone with "Grandpère." The relationship with her mother was one of mutual bitter disappointment.

Would Mother like me better if I was pretty? Amy had often wondered this, and decided not. Nothing would change Sarah Mead Delatour's hatred of Amy's French-Canadian half, nor change her resentment of Grandpère, and indeed also of the "Canuck" husband, Louis Delatour, whom Sarah had married twenty-five years ago in some unimaginable moment of reckless infatuation. She had not even wept when he died in a car crash, so long back that Amy hardly remembered her father, though there was a distant glow of ruddiness and gaiety, of French nursery songs, and of nestling tight against a warm broad chest.

The hooting blast shrilled out for the next "block," or period. Amy consulted her schedule—English now, with a new teacher, Martin Stone. An "intern" from Duke University now doing his Master's, someone had said.

Amy entered the classroom assigned for this course, settled herself in the back row of chair desks, and smiled feebly when Jeb Jones took the seat next to her.

"Hi!" she said. "D'you have a good summer?"

"Oh, great," he answered sarcastically, thudding a notebook on his desk, "hauling garbage for m' uncle. One more year and a diploma I oughta find something better, don't you think? How's yourself, Amy? You got some tan—been beaching?"

Amy sighed. "Back yard mostly. And, of course, baby sitting. Mother keeps me busy. She saves up chores." She sighed again, wishing she had any semblance of a real boy friend besides Jeb, who had tried to date her last year. Her mother's horror when she found out—for once mildly echoed by Grandpère—had stopped that. Jeb was black. Which was bad enough, but his parents were on welfare, which was worse in the eyes of both the hard-working Yankee mother and French-Canadian grandfather. Besides, Jeb was skinny and short, wore his hair in an Afro, and was given to lavender turtlenecks, always smelling slightly sour. There were few blacks in this particular high school and Jeb was as friendless as Amy, since he detested sports and viewed almost everybody with wary defiance. But they had recognized an essential loneliness in each other and been drawn into vague intimacy.

"So *that's* the guy's gonna cram English lit. into me," remarked Jeb, staring at the young teacher who had

4

slid somewhat tentatively toward the blackboard and now faced the class. "Man—is he tall!"

Amy also examined Martin Stone. He *was* extremely tall, maybe six foot three, rather thin. He looked something like a heron, Amy thought—the set of his head on the shoulders and the bright eyes peering alertly from one to another of the bored or expectant faces raised toward him, though herons did not have wavy blond hair cut into neat sideburns. Amy rebuked herself for being fanciful, as her mother always did. Mr. Stone's appraising look missed none of them, but passed quickly over Amy—she was used to that. Male eyes never lingered on her plump, triangular face, half eclipsed by unfashionable horn-rimmed spectacles.

"Good day, Class," said Martin Stone in a deep, pleasant drawl. "We'll begin with roll call."

"Stinkin' Southerner," muttered Jeb out of the corner of his mouth. "Probably queer, too, look at his fancy necktie!"

"Sh-h!" said Amy impatiently. She wasn't entirely sure what kind of "queer" Jeb meant, but she realized he was in one of his bad moods, and would dislike any white man dressed in a well-cut suit and wearing any sort of necktie. "Why'd you elect this course, anyway? You're a science nut."

"Oh, I dunno," muttered Jeb, unwilling to explain that he had been impressed by something his chemistry teacher, Mr. Brown, had said last year to the effect that successful men resulted from a well-rounded education, and that a knowledge of science alone would not produce success, that even in the modern world one needed a supplement of history and literature. Though he would rather have broken an arm than admit it, Jeb admired Mr. Brown and had felt good when he enrolled himself in this English course. Now he was regretting his impulse.

Amy jumped as she heard Mr. Stone read out her

name from a registration paper. "Amy Delatour," but he pronounced it in the French way, as Grandpère did. Her mother and everyone else called it "Delayter."

"Present," Amy said in a startled voice. Her eyes met the teacher's for a moment and she felt a shock of attraction. He had kind eyes, very penetrating, but at this distance you couldn't be sure of the color.

Martin passed on to "Drake," then began on the "Es." When he had finished the twenty or so names he made a few general remarks about literature, and handed out pamphlets on the senior English mini-course program, which was entirely elective, but he stressed the advantages of independent study if none of the regular subjects appealed. He remarked that he didn't expect anyone to make a choice overnight, but would be glad to discuss any such choices with individual students in his office at three o'clock.

Amy's heart jumped. She knew already what she wanted to study, had desperately wanted to, ever since junior high, but she was afraid of being laughed at. She half raised her hand, then lowered it, flushing, but Martin's quick eyes had caught the motion.

"Amy Delatour, you had a question?" he asked, smiling.

Several of the class turned around and stared. Doris Drake giggled. She was the prettiest girl in the school, had long straight golden hair hanging to her waist from a center part, large violet eyes and dimples. Her sudden little giggles were considered entrancing. She was a cheerleader and dated most of the "jocks" or athletes in the school. Amy envied and detested her.

"N-no, not now—" Amy said, huddling down in her seat.

Martin's heavy, straw-colored brows drew together in an inquiring frown, but he said casually, "Well, you can talk to me after school."

Jeb, who had been muttering angrily to himself as

he leafed through the pamphlet of proposed courses, said, "What did you want to ask him about *this* crap, it don't even make sense."

"Oh, nothing," answered Amy after a moment. "I guess I was just surprised he said my last name right, nobody does."

Jeb found this remark too silly for response and went on growling under his breath. Of all the books and plays mentioned, "Shakespeare" was the only name he recognized, and that because he had been one of a fairy chorus in *A Midsummer Night's Dream* put on by the seventh grade in junior high.

When Amy presented herself at Martin Stone's office that afternoon she was so nervous that her hands trembled and she looked sulky from the effort to control the quivering of her mouth. But both her strong desire and inherited doggedness forced her to appear.

Martin stood up when she entered, a gallantry she had never encountered, and motioned her to a chair on the other side of his desk.

He had rapidly looked up Amy's grades before she came and found them extremely good. The "confidential" teachers' report was less glowing, and he had not yet finished it. "Seems to have no friends or social instincts. Withdrawn. Difficult to 'reach.' Home situation poor, by inference. Nobody ever appears at PTA meetings and the mother not co-operative. (See eighth grade reports.) Superior scholarly aptitude, but an unattractive personality."

The latter wasn't quite true, Martin thought. Too damning. The girl, if she lost several pounds, let her abundant reddish brown hair fall loose instead of skewered in a bun in back, and if she stopped hunching herself defensively, *might* be attractive. She wore faded blue jeans like most of them, and a hideously shapeless T shirt, but at least her clothes looked clean.

"Amy," he said abruptly, but with the warm smile

7

she already found comforting, "would you take your glasses off a moment, or do you really need them all the time to see?"

She was so startled that her hands stopped trembling and she gave an uncertain little laugh. "I'm near-sighted," she said, "I read so much, but I guess I don't need 'em *all* the time." She took off her thick spectacles and he was agreeably surprised. The eyes were large, thick-lashed, and of a clear shining gray.

"Thanks," he said. "I'm delighted that you read a lot. So you'll have no trouble choosing a mini-course, or independent study?"

"I *have* chosen a subject of my own—if you'll let me. It's—it's not like any on the list." She twisted her fingers together and jerked up her chin.

"Well, what is this subject?"

She took a deep breath and spoke in a rush. "Henry Wadsworth Longfellow, with special reference to *Evangeline,* which he got all *wrong.*"

"What!" Martin could not help laughing. "My dear girl! Longfellow! You had him in junior high, didn't you? And what do you mean he got *Evangeline* all wrong, though he did in a way, I suppose, but that's poetic license. And anyhow, Longfellow was rather a bland, square type, how could you really find him interesting?"

"He wasn't *really* square! He lived in Europe for ages, he spoke and translated from seven or eight languages. He was nervous and shy inside, he had lots of miserable times, and then awful tragedies. His first wife died pregnant in Holland; his baby girl died; and his second wife, whom he adored, got burned up when her hoopskirt caught fire." Amy inhaled sharply. "He nearly died himself trying to rescue her—so brave to go near the—the flames. *I* couldn't have."

"Well—" said Martin, amused, also puzzled by the

8

shuddering way she said, "flames." "How do you know all this?"

"I've read every biography of Longfellow I can find in our school library and the public library too," Amy said earnestly. "And all his poems, I love *Hiawatha* because I love Indians. He got the right feel there, but he's all wrong about *Evangeline*."

Martin leaned back in his chair and carefully lit his pipe, giving himself time to assess the girl's transformation from a dumpy, fidgety little owl to a creature of passionate conviction. But imagine any adolescent in this day and age falling in love with Longfellow, or being so involved with *any* intellectual project for that matter! There were mysteries about this plain little girl.

"I knew you'd laugh at me and say 'no,' " said Amy suddenly collapsing and turning a dull red.

Martin drew on his pipe and watched the smoke curl up to the brightly lit ceiling. "I'm not laughing, Amy. I'm interested. Have you known any Indians?"

She shook her head. "Only in—well—dreams. I've never been away from around Greenwich, except I hitched to Cambridge last summer to see Craigie House where Longfellow lived—my mother was furious. She thinks—thinks I'm nuts anyway, though Grandpère doesn't."

"Grandpère," repeated Martin. "Is he French?"

"Of course," said Amy. "French-Canadian. We always talk French together, though Mother hates it. I was wondering, Mr. Stone, how come you pronounced my name right?"

"Because," said Martin, "I'm from New Orleans and my mother is a Creole. That, by the way, means pure French or Spanish blood in Louisiana; mother's line is mostly French. She was born at a plantation called Bellerive, near New Iberia in the bayous, where there is a lot of French spoken. Where did your grandfather come from?"

"Acadie," said Amy, her eyes kindling again. "Nova Scotia it's called *now,* but he moved to Rivière du Loup in Quebec as a young man. Oh, Mr. Stone, I *knew* you were different from the Yankees. Perhaps we're related way back, so many of the poor Acadians went to Louisiana when the Yankees and the British kicked them out of their homes in Nova Scotia. They call them 'Cajuns' now. Grandpère has told me a lot about the old days, as he heard it from *his* grandparents and back and back, sometimes I 'dream true' about it. I almost feel I *lived* then. Anyway, my ancestress was the *real* Evangeline I think. Her name was Ange-Marie, and so is mine. My mother shortened it to 'Amy' after I was baptized." She subsided suddenly, twisting her hands. She had never made such a long speech to anyone.

Martin said, "I see—" in a musing voice, "but my mother wasn't a Cajun, her people came from France years later, so I guess we're not related, Amy, though I do know some French and am definitely *not* a Yankee." He chuckled and reverted to her startling statement.

"So you think your ancestress might be the *real* Evangeline? In the Cajun country, they do have a story different from Longfellow's. They think the girl was actually called Emmeline LaBiche, and that she died of a broken heart at St. Martinville on Bayou Teche. Died when the lover she searched for so long turned up married to someone else."

"There wasn't any Emmeline LaBiche in *Acadia,* at least in Grand Pré," said Amy with a flat certainty, which both astounded him and made him uneasy.

This is peculiar, he thought, for the large gray eyes held a faraway listening look, as though she heard something he could not. "Well," he said, "when the whole Acadian population was forcibly exiled from

10

Nova Scotia, families torn apart and put on separate ships, there were doubtless many poor lovers who lost each other, and doubtless several unhappy girls who plodded for years in search of their sweethearts, or husbands. It was a cruel act the British and Yankees perpetrated long ago—1755, wasn't it?"

"I guess so," she said dully. "There was cruelty, heartbreak—and fire."

"So Longfellow got *that* much right, anyway," he said smiling, though he was still uneasy, and somewhat intrigued. Amy had put on her glasses, and subsided suddenly into a plain dumpy girl, who was scuffing her sneakers, and gnawing on a fingernail.

Martin glanced at his wristwatch. "Oh Lord, I'm late for a teachers' meeting, I'll think about your project, and I'd like to know more about you. Have you written your requested autobiography during the last two years here?"

Amy shook her head. "I didn't want to, it's so boring." The corners of her pink mouth drooped.

"Will you write it for me, Amy?" he asked gently. "Put everything in, the 'dreaming true,' as well."

She hesitated, hunching down in her chair, but he was standing by the door, holding it open for her. She walked out, her footsteps dragging, unreasonably hurt by this dismissal. She had missed her usual bus and walked over two miles home to the hot, cramped rooms above a delicatessen on Greenwich Avenue. She climbed the stairs and, to her surprise, found the door unlocked. It was still too early for her mother to be back from the Stamford department store where she worked as a clerk. And too early for Grandpère to have shut his struggling little woodwork shop in Cos Cob. He always stayed there until six, just in case there might be a customer for his beautifully carved boxes, his stools, his chests, or there might even be a refinishing job asked for. But the customers dwindled yearly.

Amy shrugged off the little puzzle of the unlocked door and set about getting supper as usual, when she heard a frightening sound from her grandfather's room. It was a groaning, choking noise.

She ran into his room and found him gasping on the bed. His brown leathery face was sweating where it wasn't covered by grizzled mustache and beard, and he clawed frantically at his chest.

"Grandpère!" Amy cried, rushing over to him. She tore his collar open. He gasped again and subsided on the high stacked pillows, his gnarled hands falling limp.

"*Maman—Maman, viens m'aider—*" he whispered in a thin frightened voice.

Amid her panic Amy felt wondering pity that the old man should be calling for his mother, so long dead. She dipped a corner of his sheet in the pitcher of water he always kept on his night stand, began distractedly to mop his face and neck, down to the great chest with its mat of coarse white hair.

In a moment Pierre Delatour's color became normal, his breathing grew even, and she saw the chest where the heart had been thumping erratically, grow quiet. "*Ah, ma chérie,*" he whispered and turned his head so that his cheek lay against her hand.

"But what *happened*, Grandpère?" she asked him in French. "You looked terrible."

He shrugged, pointing to his breastbone, then closing his eyes wearily, suddenly fell asleep.

Heart attack? thought Amy, what'll I do? Doctor? But who? They hadn't had a doctor since she was a baby. Hospital, then, they took people to the Emergency Room now, she had heard some of the girls talking about it in the gym locker.

Amy suddenly realized that her mother's footsteps were thudding around outside, and for once she was glad. She gently detached her hand from under her grandfather's cheek and hurried to the kitchen. "Oh,

12

Mother, Grandpère's had some sort of bad attack, he couldn't breathe, he turned gray. I was so frightened."

Sarah Mead Delatour compressed her thin lips and said, "The old fool, won't realize he's near to eighty. I expect he's been heaving around those fancy chests he carves—and never sells."

"But, Mother, he tries so hard to help out—and, Mother, he's *sick,* shouldn't we have a doctor?"

Sarah sniffed. In September she had allergies, but the sniff was a long-time habit which annoyed her daughter. There had never been tenderness between them, only duty. The tenderness Amy had received as a child came from the bluff, laughing French-Canadian father —and Grandpère. *They* played with her, and let her climb on their muscular thighs, and sometimes rocked her to sleep. But her father, Louis, had been killed in the car crash when she was eight, "full of beer, as usual," said Sarah, and otherwise spoke not at all about him. Sarah shed no public tears even when the official notice came that her eldest, Edward, had been killed in Vietnam four years ago. But Amy knew very well that her mother deeply regretted that the Lord had taken Edward instead of Amy.

"Mind you scrub the potatoes *thoroughly,*" Sarah said, "and wash the lettuce, and don't you go a-trying to make a frenchified dressing again. Takes too much oil. I suppose I must have a look at Mr. Delayter," which was the only way she ever addressed her father-in-law. She squared her thin shoulders under the navy blue and white nylon print she wore in the store and entered Grandpère's room. She came out in a minute. "Sleeping," she said. "Look's OK to me. Those Canucks are all alike. Make fusses over nothing."

"He *doesn't!*" cried Amy, her eyes flashing behind her glasses. "You know he doesn't. And he was awfully sick. Mother, you're so damn unfair to him!"

"Well, I must say"—Sarah inhaled sharply—"swear

13

words now—if you were younger I'd wash your mouth out with soap. How dare you talk to me like that! Oh, I know how you and your grandpa stick together, jabbering that silly language so I won't understand. And what about *me,* on my feet eight hours a day selling fancy stuff to a lot of la-di-da women, just so us and *him* can eat. You're old enough to work full time, I've a mind to take you out of that high school where you mix with a lot of riffraff, yes, I really think—" Sarah was working herself up into a querulous anger, born of hay fever, a nagging pain in her leg, and the general futility of her lot. But Amy interrupted her vehemently.

"I get very good grades, Mother, you've got to admit!"

"That's the Mead part of you, though precious little else *is,* and I rue the day I said 'Yes,' to your father, and now I'm saddled with *him.*" She jerked her head toward Grandpère's room, "And with—"

"Me," Amy said through her teeth. "I'm sorry you don't like me."

Sarah flinched. True or not, those were feelings never to be admitted. And what had come over Amy? Talking back, downright rude! Sarah gave a prolonged sniffle and wiped her dripping red nose on her handkerchief. "Lay the table!" she said. "And no sulks either." She went and, turning on the gas burner, poured the remnants of yesterday's stew into a saucepan. If Edward had only lived, she thought, the long suppressed lump rising in her throat, Edward had been *all* Mead. She saw his steady blue eyes, his serious smile, and heard the way he called her "Ma." Edward had never reminded her of Louis Delatour. Edward wouldn't even learn French, try as they would, those two Canucks, father and son—to make him. Edward, so mangled by the bomb that killed him that she had never opened the small box of remains, which had been buried near the Mead plot in Putnam Cemetery. Mr. Delayter had

14

demanded a Roman Catholic ceremony, but she had bested the old man *there*. She savagely stirred the mess in the saucepan, remembering the time she had snatched a rosary away from Amy and spanked her with a hairbrush, knowing very well who had given it to the child.

Mother and daughter sat down and ate in silence. When the scanty tasteless meal ended Amy went in to check on her grandfather. He was sitting up against the pillows and greeted her with a loving wistful smile. "Ange-Marie," he whispered, his bluish lips lingering over the name which Sarah found so ridiculous. "Angel-Mary," she never would have permitted such an outlandish name to be given the baby daughter had she not been very ill for some weeks after Amy's birth.

The girl bent over and kissed her grandfather on the cheek. He always smelled of pine shavings and cheap tobacco, from a little clay pipe he puffed on at work. Sarah permitted no smoking in her home.

"*Ça va mieux—*" he said, and went on to tell Amy that his attack was nothing, she must not worry, and he hoped that her mother had not been perturbed. He always treated his daughter-in-law with meticulous courtesy though he knew that she loathed him.

Amy hastened to reassure, when Sarah stalked in.

"So you've finished your nap," she said sharply. "Hungry now, I guess—" Her faded watery eyes narrowed as she saw that Amy was actually stroking the old man's head.

"A leetle bit 'ongry," said Pierre Delatour apologetically.

"We can spare some milk," said Sarah. "Amy'll bring it, no doubt, if you don't feel like be-stirring *yourself*."

"Thank you," he said, but his voice quavered and an unhealthy flush spread over his bearded cheeks. "I 'ave not yet regained all my forces."

15

Sarah sniffed, and going to her bedroom, slammed the door shut.

Amy tended to her grandfather. The heat was stifling in the little flat. She brought the kitchen electric fan to his room, and he sighed gratefully as he felt the air move over him.

The stifling weight of hostility was not so easily dissipated. Like the vapors from a stagnant swamp it penetrated and poisoned each of the four small rooms. Amy went to her own cubicle, which overlooked a parking lot. The air always smelled of gasoline and asphalt, and, in this weather, the stench of overflowing garbage pails from the delicatessen below. She undressed and lay down on her cot. She had a picture of Longfellow on the wall, the strong bearded face always looked to her like her grandfather. The other picture was a seascape, with roaring breakers on a rocky coast. Amy had never seen the real sea, but she loved the picture.

She shut her eyes and immediately thought of the new English teacher. Of the extraordinary fact that he had spent so much time with her; still more extraordinary that she had really talked to him and told him some of her heart's secrets. He had even asked her to tell about what she called "dreaming true," and didn't *seem* to be making fun of her. Could I try it tonight? she thought.

There was comfort and beauty in the dream, when it came—until the fear set in. There was a ritual to make the dream come, though it didn't always work.

Amy crossed her ankles and put her clasped hands under her head, while repeating a verse of Longfellow's adapted for herself, from the first poem of his she had read in sixth grade.

Often I think of the beautiful town
That is seated by the sea . . .

*And a verse of a Lapland song is haunting my
    memory still—
A girl's will is the wind's will,
And the thoughts of youth are long, long
    thoughts . . .*

Tonight the incantation succeeded. Almost at once
she could smell a salty tang in the air, hear the distant
lapping of tidewater as it filled a bay, see sturdy
thatched houses on a village street with a hill behind,
and a tall church spire roofed with wooden shingles
enclosing a large iron bell. In her right hand she felt
the wicker handle of a woven basket and knew that
there were fresh-baked loaves of bread in the basket.
They smelled delicious. The sun was rising above the
distant water and the nearby meadows, gilding the
tall grain which rippled like a river in the fresh breeze.
She was walking to one of the houses, and she heard
her steps make clop-clopping, wooden sounds on the
roughly cobbled street. Ahead, in the house where she
was bound, there would be a hearth fire, for it was
chilly in the dawning, and inside that special house
would be warmth, laughter, and welcoming kisses
from all its big family. There would also be Paul.

A yearning love possessed her, and a passion of
homesickness so strong that her actual heart thumped
as hard as had poor Grandpère's this afternoon. The
thumping broke the dream before it went on to panic
and loss—to angry voices and scarlet tongues of con-
suming flame.

Amy uncrossed her sweat-sticky ankles and sat up
suddenly. "You're an idiot, Amy," she said. "That
couldn't be Longfellow's town. *That* was Portland,
Maine, he was writing about. My village isn't Portland."
Where then? No place but in dreams. She remembered
again a conversation about herself between two eighth-
grade teachers which she had overheard.

17

"That Amy Delayter—remarkable imagination—judging from her themes, but something queer about the child, out of touch with reality—I hope not schizophrenic. We'd better have the psychologist look at her —psychiatric clinic—"

The rest was blurred because she had been so frightened. There was a pleasant woman who questioned, gave her lots of tests, which she must have passed since nothing happened, except that her mother was summoned to the school, went angrily and returned contemptuously.

"They don't know whether you're crazy or not—the nerve of them! I told them a thing or two and left them dithering. They said you had a very high I.Q., whatever *that* is. Mind, you stop *acting* crazy, or you'll be shut up in a padded cell somewhere!"

After that Amy never again mentioned her dream life to anyone, even Grandpère. But she *had* to Martin Stone. Oh, *why* had she! She knew now what "schizophrenia" meant. She had looked it up in the dictionary. Perhaps Mr. Stone thought her abnormal, too, and would—after stringing her along—send her back to the psychiatric clinic. I wish I was dead, Amy whispered, though she couldn't really imagine death.

She tossed on the cot, trying to find a cool spot, and finally fell into restless sleep.

The next day there was a breeze, and Amy's spirits were improved enough to endure the morning hassle of getting all three of them to their respective buses. Grandpère, although obviously weak, insisted on returning to his tiny shop, for there was one commission waiting. An eccentric old lady from back-country Greenwich wanted a hand-made dog kennel for her Irish wolfhound, and had discovered Pierre Delatour by accident while going to a lobster wharf in Cos Cob. She would pay no more than fifty dollars for the kennel still, fifty dollars would help out.

They all three choked down stale Danish pastry, which came cheap from the deli below, and some coffee. All three ate in silence until time for the usual argument about Amy's lunch money. Sarah always grumbled about doling out sixty cents. "You eat too much anyway," she said to her daughter. "You're fat. Tomorrow you'll take left-over sandwiches from home. I can't afford all these cafeteria splurges." Amy scarcely listened, so accustomed was she to the complaints. She caught her bus after a short walk and found herself looking forward to school. To seeing Martin Stone. Actually, except for the much-hated compulsory gym, where she was always more awkward and slower than the other girls and felt that her figure was grotesque, her classes held no terrors. French was and always had been a breeze, although her accent was different from the teacher's. Some loyalty to her grandfather and innate promptings had made her take art in the form of handicrafts. It was too soon to know if she had aptitude, but she had found pleasure in molding clay for a pot, and in the whir of the potter's wheel. She looked forward to decorating and glazing the pot. Then there was English, which gave her an anxious excitement.

Thank God, math was forever behind her; she had hated it all the years it was required, and, in those courses only, had even once dropped to a C.

The English "block" came late in the morning today. She sidled nervously into the same back seat, absently noting that Jeb was again in the next one. Mr. Stone came in and surveyed the class. She flushed as he gave her a tiny nod, but she saw with dismay that his eyes stopped on Doris Drake, who sat in the front row and looked remarkably pretty in a rose-colored mini-dress, with her shining blond hair held back by a pink bow.

Even from where she sat Amy could see the long eyelashes fluttering, the arching of Doris's lush bra-less breasts. The girl gave out an aura of sex which infuriated Amy. What male could resist it? And, unfortunately, despite her giggles and her air of fluffy dependence, Amy knew that Doris was a good student.

Martin was more informal today, having inspected the other teachers; his sport shirt was open at the neck, he wore no tie, and his manner was less constrained. He was speaking again about the independent studies. "One of you has already approached me with a subject, which I must say I found quite original, but this school permits more latitude for individual choices than other schools I've known. Has anyone else decided on a subject for my consideration?"

Three hands went up, one of them Jeb's.

Martin nodded in his direction. "Yes, Jeb."

"I want to study black scientists, what they've done an' their writings. *All* of 'em, from the beginning," said Jeb, chewing gum rapidly in his embarrassment. "I can find out the names, I guess." He subsided with a grunt and cocked his head defiantly.

Martin smiled. "Perfectly laudable and perfectly feasible," he said, then seeing blankness on the intelligent dark face he added quickly, "Great idea, Jeb, I'm sure the committee will pass it."

Jeb relaxed. "He ain't so bad," he murmured to Amy, and began to whistle through his teeth.

Somebody wanted to do "creative writing"; Doris Drake in her caressing little girl voice said she'd like to do Shakespeare's heroines to tie in with her drama course, where she rather guessed she could do some acting, too. "Like Ophelia or Imogen, Mr. Stone," she said with charming assurance. "Can't you just see me as Imogen?" she asked, smiling up at him seductively and sure of a compliment.

Martin was amused. He'd been warned about this little sexpot, who had caused trouble last year and whose expectation of desirous masculine reactions was seldom disappointed. Even among the male teach-

20

ers, he'd heard. "A delightful Imogen, I'm sure," said Martin in a neutral voice, and went on at once to outline the courses.

Amy's optimism slowly ebbed. She began to see how ridiculous her own project was, she lost confidence in it. And the few moments of intimacy in Mr. Stone's office yesterday seemed unreal. Nor could she ask for another interview so soon. Already he was making appointments with several students. It was as though a door had opened a crack and then banged shut. Since the nod of recognition he had never looked in her direction. After class she trailed out with the others to the Student Center, which was, as usual, very noisy. Two boys were setting off firecrackers in a corner of the enormous hall. Another pair were engaged in a wrestling match. Although a monitor tried to keep order, sheer numbers outweighed him. Over a thousand young people were in high spirits, enjoying their lunch period. Amy saw Doris in the corner by the east windows holding court. One of the boys on the football team, Mac Wilton, was plunking a guitar and languidly singing to Doris, *"Oh, baby, what you going to give me, Oh, baby, let's make it good, us two."* He was a handsome dark-haired lad, and one of the most popular "jocks" in the school. He also had a sexy Elvis Presley voice.

It was Doris's pretty way to reward her admirers lavishly. She rubbed her cheek against that of Mac Wilton and gave him a long clinging kiss.

Nobody spoke to Amy beyond an indifferent "Hi, there!" She drifted to the jammed cafeteria and spent all her lunch money on cokes and ice cream. She was miserable.

Later, during an open block, she went to her homeroom and tried to write the autobiography Mr. Stone had asked for. She covered one page with her neat

21

legible writing, then stopped. What was there to say after the beginning, "I was born in Greenwich Hospital March 13th 1957. I had an older brother, Edward. He was killed in Vietnam. My father, Louis Delatour, was killed in an automobile accident when I was eight. I live with my mother, Sarah Mead Delatour, whose family has been in Greenwich over three hundred years. Also, I live with my grandfather, Pierre Delatour. He and my father were cabinetmakers from Quebec Province. 'Ménuisier' is the French word for cabinetmaker. They came south to the States from Rivière du Loup, looking for better pay, and found it. In the early fifties quite a lot of Greenwich people wanted fine woodwork done. We used to live in a pretty little house near the Mianus River. Now we have four rooms over a delicatessen." And what else *was* there? She certainly was not going to tell him again about her "other life" or about the "dreaming true" which she had so foolishly mentioned. She folded the sheet, marking it, "For Mr. Stone from Amy Delatour," and put it in her tote bag to be delivered tomorrow. She left the building and made for her bus, which, through some miscalculation, was already full and pulled away as she reached it.

She stood disconsolately on the sidewalk for a moment. Other belated students either had cars or bicycles or would be picked up by their mothers. Amy must walk again or wait for the four o'clock bus and the afternoon had grown very hot.

Martin Stone was quitting the school grounds in his little VW when he saw Amy on the sidewalk and the forlorn expression of her unguarded face touched him.

He drew up beside her. "Do you want a lift, Amy?" Her bewildered expression turned to a tremulous smile, incredulity and joy were transparent to him. Poor child, he thought, she has no defenses. A crusading spirit edged into his consciousness, mingled with caution, but it was something to see anybody's face light up like that so candidly. Martin was twenty-six and had had his share of affairs in college at Tulane, at Duke, and particularly later during the ghastly year and a half near Saigon which he usually managed to forget. But no woman had reacted to him quite as spontaneously as this!

She silently clambered into the seat beside him. "Thanks," she said, staring straight ahead through the windshield. "And I hope it's not out of your way. I live 'way down on Greenwich Avenue."

"Not at all," he said, smiling. "I've a little apartment quite near you on Steamboat Road myself. But it's early yet and I want to talk to you. Let's go to the beach for a while—Greenwich Point, maybe?"

"I've no beach card," she said. "Mother considers them a useless extravagance. Besides, I have to start supper. There's stewing lamb Mother got cheap because it was getting a bit smelly," she added ingenuously.

Martin formed an immediate, nearly accurate impression of the girl's mother.

"Do you ever have any fun, Amy?" he asked impulsively.

"I guess not," she answered slowly, looking startled, "except my books from the library, of course *we* don't have a TV."

Martin grunted and rapidly considered taking her to a beach and paying her entrance fee, then realized that there would be talk if they were seen there, despite Amy's obvious lack of seductiveness.

"Tell you what—" he said, "we can park a while at the end of Steamboat Road, right by the Sound—look at the boats. The smelly lamb won't get any 'higher' in half an hour and I really want to ask you a few things about your project."

She made a quaintly dignified little nod and said nothing as they drove down Greenwich Avenue on to

Steamboat Road. He drew up at the dead end next to the Indian Harbor Yacht Club property and said, "Have you written your bio for me?"

"Yes. There isn't much." She drew the folded sheet of paper from her tote bag.

He read it fast and frowned. "This tells me nothing about yourself except that the deaths of your father and brother must have been shocking blows, very traumatic. What about *you*, your dreams, your ambitions, what do you want to make of your life?"

"I don't know." She hunched down in the seat and laced her fingers nervously. He noted that she had rather pretty hands, small, square palmed, but long fingered, except that the nails had been bitten down to the quick. All the tremulous joy had left her, she looked sulky and embarrassed and Martin was moved by both of his intellectual sides—the born teacher's desire to bring out talent, and his absorption in psychology. The latter had been growing since he went to Duke and he had decided to switch his field to psychology once this English-teaching year was over. There was no hurry.

Martin was financially comfortable due to an inheritance from his recently deceased father, Judge Stone, who had been a celebrated and wealthy lawyer in New Orleans. Amy constituted a psychological problem which he wished to solve. He also wished to help anyone so obviously living in unhappy limbo. "Turn around and smile, Amy," he commanded. "You have a nice smile when you let it loose."

She was so surprised that she obeyed with a half-hysterical gulp. "That's better," he said, smiling back at her. "Now take off those hideous glasses and let your hair down—literally, I mean. No girl your age wears a tight old granny knot like that."

He bolstered his command with an intent, steady gaze and she obeyed again, pulling heavy hair pins from her hair and shaking the reddest chestnut mass around her shoulders, although she was pink with embarrassment. "I—I believe you're hypnotizing me," she said, trying to laugh. "Mother doesn't like me to look like this."

"Never mind," cut in Martin, gaining further insight into the probably jealous rigidities of Mrs. Delatour. "You've no idea how the long hair improves you. As to hypnotism—I wasn't—but I *could,* I think. Bright people make the best subjects."

"You mean you can *do* it?" Amy forgot herself in her astonishment.

"Virtually anybody can learn to 'do' it," he said, laughing, "but I've taken a course, also have studied para-psychology."

"What's that?" Her gray eyes widened.

"Fringe sciences—nonverbal communication, extrasensory perception, psycho-kinetics, meditation, hypnotism, and the like. Some people call these the 'lunatic fringe,' except that hypnotism has become a recognized psychiatric tool. Listen, Amy, you've got me off the track. I want to talk about your really extraordinary enthusiasm for Longfellow. I reread some of him last night and he isn't very good, my dear, by modern standards. His most famous short poem, *The Psalm of Life*"—Martin shook his head—" 'Tell me not in mournful numbers, Life is but an empty dream, For the soul is dead that slumbers, And things are not what they seem. . . .' That's practically doggerel."

"Oh, I suppose—" she said, drooping, "I knew you wouldn't let me. I'm not sure myself now. It was just that some of the things he wrote seemed to be meant for *me*. *Evangeline* when I first read it had a lovely glow, and yet made me uncomfortable because that *wasn't* the way it was. I keep wanting to tell the *true* story—and another thing, you know *My Lost Youth?*"

"Yes," said Martin, "the old boy did better on that

one, but you haven't any 'lost youth,' you've hardly begun on 'youth' at all." He quirked his eyebrows.

"But I have a lost youth," said Amy, very seriously, "not this one, another one."

"Do you feel that when you 'dream true'?" asked Martin quietly, after a moment.

"Yes, yes—I do," she cried. "Now laugh all you want to!"

Martin did not laugh. He was puzzled again, although aware of possible dangers to her in a fantasy life. Aware, too, of that distressing little item in her eighth-grade report—"some apparent abnormality, especially pyrophobia—got hysterical during a fire drill. Thoroughly tested for schizophrenia, but diagnosis seemed negative." Still, that was four years ago and if she's clinically schizoid, I'll eat my diplomas.

He lit his pipe and puffed on it while they both gazed silently at the pleasure boats scudding around the sparkling harbor.

After a while he spoke, "It seems to me that from what little I know of you, that instead of Longfellow, you might explore the ethnic group with which you obviously identify. Take 'The French-speaking Peoples of North America.' How would you like *that?* I could find you the best Louisiana books for the Cajuns."

"Maybe—" said Amy reluctantly after a moment. "I hate to tell about it. There's a wall. I mean—" She stopped, afraid of saying too much again, but his kind gaze was encouraging. "I mean that though I love the French side of me and I love speaking it with Grandpère, still in dreams, after the happy parts in the beginning, there is so much pain and fear, and then fire—I'm so afraid of fire—"

"H-mmm," said Martin thoughtfully. "You're afraid of the dream fears. Do they wake you up?" She nodded while her lips tightened. "But you *know* the fears aren't
26

real, just something in your unconscious—much better to let them out."

The girl turned her head away from him, her near-sighted eyes vaguely watching the multicolored spinnakers, homecoming on a light breeze.

"It's all as real as you are," she said in a voice so low that he strained to hear.

Martin swallowed. Her own conviction impressed him uncomfortably. He looked at his wristwatch. "I must get you home," he said. "But we'll talk again soon, won't we?"

He was surprised to find how much he wanted to talk to her again. It was not only that he liked the girl, and felt in her a mysterious need, but he was excited at the thought of an experiment—if it could be managed without embarrassing either of them.

He had turned the car and they were passing the building on the harbor where he had a pleasant water-view apartment. He glanced toward it, frowning. No, not so soon—could make trouble, and even in this permissive age somebody might jump to the wrong conclusion.

He realized that Amy had not answered him, as she twisted her hair back into the ugly bun, and put on her glasses.

"Don't you want to talk with me again?" he asked, half laughing, half rueful, wondering if he had imagined the joy in her face when he offered her a lift.

"Not if you think I'm crazy," she said. "You make me say things I don't want to and I guess you'll report them all to the guidance counselor. Here"—she broke off, pointing to a squat brownish building—"over there's where I live. Thanks a lot." She was out of the car even as he looked for a parking space. She disappeared, running like a clumsy young colt.

Martin drove slowly back to his apartment and, shoving aside for the present the mass of school

27

papers and schedules he had brought home in his brief-case, he went to a corner bookshelf in his living room. There he kept his books on hypnotism and parapsychology.

Chapter Two

It was nearly two weeks before Amy and Martin's adventure began in a clandestine way which bothered Martin, though he saw no way of avoiding secrecy, but did not perturb Amy at all.

On a Thursday evening, when the first maples were turning, and a bluish haze drifted over the Sound, Amy walked down Greenwich Avenue to Steamboat Road and knocked at the door of Martin's ground floor apartment, as they had agreed. The meeting had been simple to arrange; there were always conferences between teachers and students, and even in their assigned house—one of the four units, each like a separate high school within the big one—there were so many people coming and going to so many classes that particular conferences were not noticed. Amy had made scant impression on her housemaster or the guidance counselor; she was quiet, well behaved, and clearly in no academic difficulties. The counselors had plenty of immediate problems to cope with, ranging from pot-smoking and beer drinking in the bushes, to rebellious youngsters who disliked their electives, or hated a teacher, or simply played hooky.

In theory, teachers and students *might* meet after hours; the school, naturally, did not supervise their private lives, yet there were unwritten rules, and Amy was only sixteen. Martin was a trifle embarrassed when the girl duly appeared on his doorstep. "No trouble at home?" he asked, tapping his pipe against the door jamb.

"Oh no," said Amy. "Mother works late Thursdays at the store, Grandpère, too, he's finishing that kennel for old Mrs. Riston. Anyway, I go out nights baby sitting very often. I'm anxious for the experiment you spoke about. Will it be hard?"

"Don't know," said Martin. "May not work at all." He motioned her into the living room.

It was a charming room. The west side had glass doors opening onto a minute balcony over the cove. The lap of water was clear. His furnishings were simple, but bright with color, quite modern except for an heirloom ruby glass chandelier he had brought from New Orleans. It hung over a round lucite table, littered with papers. There were contour chairs, a divan covered with a soft Navajo blanket, a pickled wood desk, and two high bookcases. Martin's solitary picture was a dreamy, sensuous Chagall, outstanding against a gray-blue wall. His heavy shag rug was white.

"What a—a nice place," said Amy. "I've never seen anything like it." She was aware of the room's fragrance, a compound of pipe smoke, dried rose leaves in a bowl, and salt air. She was happy to be there. She settled in a chair with a little satisfied sigh, and looked expectant.

Martin pulled down the shades against the setting sun, and turned on his stereo. He had picked the music carefully. An album of French songs, slow in rhythm, and was suddenly wryly conscious of how much this resembled a classic seduction scene, which annoyed him, though he knew that Amy was far too innocent for any such thoughts.

"Have a Coke?" he asked crisply, and brought it to her when she nodded.

He sat down in the other chair. "How's Longfellow

getting on?" he asked, because he was reluctant to begin. "And I'm pleased that you're taking my Chaucer course as well as your own project. I suppose you want the credits—mean to graduate early?"

Amy smiled. "I hope so," she said. "Mother can't wait for me to get a full-time job, we're so broke, but she won't let me check at the supermarkets, she's funny like that, and anyway, I'm terrible at figures." She added suddenly, "But mostly I like to hear you teach, it thrills me."

Martin cleared his throat. He noted that she had taken her glasses off and was looking at him with the transparently admiring gaze. This won't do at all, he thought. Kids were always getting crushes on teachers and what a dowdy kid this was after all. Except for her fine eyes she looked like a shabby little bag of potatoes, and she scuffed her worn sneakers against each other in a most irritating way.

"Look, Amy," he said, "I'm maybe foolish to ask you here, but I want to try something. I want to make it very clear that it has nothing to do with you being a girl and me a man. And I want you to trust me completely and impersonally. Now, do these French songs mean anything to you? Please listen."

She looked puzzled, then complied, cocking her head thoughtfully. "They're pretty," she said, "all about love, but the accent isn't like mine and there are some words I don't know."

He nodded. "You speak a Canadian French, which started in Normandy centuries ago. But I hoped the songs 'd put you in a dreamy mood. I want to explore your dreams."

"OK," she said, with some reluctance. "But how?"

"Hypnosis," he answered flatly. "I've studied it, as I told you, and it can open remarkable layers of consciousness. Will you give it a try?"

She nodded slowly.

31

He reached below the table and turned on his tape recorder.

"Lean back," he said, "and stare up at the little bulb in that ruby glass chandelier. You will soon get very sleepy. Relax, relax your face muscles, let them go. Relax your arms, your legs. You're getting sleepier . . ." He went on quietly in a soothing monotonous voice, watching the girl gradually grow limp.

She lay still with her head on the chair back, staring at the chandelier. Good subject, he thought. He continued talking until he thought her ready for the first test. "Now you can *not* lift your left arm from your lap. You may try, but you can't, not before I tell you to."

He saw her arm tremble with the effort to move, then go limp again. "*Now* you *may* raise your left arm," he said. She raised it slowly. "Shut your eyes," said Martin. She did so. "Now you are asleep," he said. "You hear what I say, but you won't remember. I want you to tell me about the 'dreaming true.' Go there, to that place, and report what you see."

To his dismay she began to squirm, her head moved from side to side in a "no" gesture.

"What's the matter?" asked Martin carefully. "You said you'd tell me about your special dream. Speak, Amy!"

Her agitation grew more pronounced, her lips clamped themselves together after emitting a strangled, "No."

He viewed this resistance with some alarm. In the hundreds of cases he had watched and the scores he had hypnotized himself he had never seen a subject go so deep and then refuse co-operation.

"Are you afraid, Amy?" he asked in a neutral voice. She did not answer, but he saw sweat break out on her round forehead. "Are you afraid of *me?*" he persisted.

She gave a slight shake of her head. "You're afraid of the dream . . . ? Can't you speak, Amy?"

She made a great effort and whispered, "You didn't start right." He had to lean close to hear her.

"Something I should say . . . ? What is it . . . ?"

"Wind's will . . ." she whispered in a faint sighing voice. Suddenly her face altered, it became softer, more alluring. She opened her eyes wide and stared at him. *"C'est que je cherche mon amour, mais le feu va nous séparer. L'incendie . . ."*

Martin's spine prickled, the change was so sudden, for now there was fright in the wide-staring eyes that did not see him and then the vehement rush of almost archaic French which came out in a deeper voice than Amy's normal one.

"It's time you woke up, Amy," he said with authority. "I'll count to ten and at the count of ten I'll snap my fingers and you'll awaken. One . . . two . . ."

He was greatly relieved when she obeyed. The wild strange light left her fixed gaze, her eyelids drooped. She put her hand to her forehead and stared blankly at the moisture on her fingers. She gave a nervous laugh. "It didn't work, did it?" she said apologetically. "Why am I perspiring? It's so hot. Would you open the windows?"

"Something worked," said Martin dryly. "Do you remember anything?"

She shook her head. "I'm sorry to be disappointing," she spoke in a small unhappy tone. "I guess that's the way I am."

"Nonsense!" said Martin, filled with pity and guilt. His psychology professor at Duke had warned against the irresponsible practice of hypnotism and particularly of using it as a parlor trick. But I *wasn't*, Martin answered himself. I want to help Amy, bring her out, release her from her fears. It's a scientific experiment. Claire would understand, he thought suddenly. Martin had a warm, relieved feeling when he thought of Claire, who had been in his psychology class and was only a year older, although she already had her Ph.D. and was teaching emotionally disturbed children in New York. Must phone Claire, he thought, haven't seen her in too long.

Amy was dejectedly putting on her glasses. "I guess I'd better go."

"No, wait . . ." Martin shook himself and temporarily dismissed Claire. "You didn't fail in any way. Perhaps I did. I think you should listen to the tape. I'll play it back."

She subsided with a worried frown, and putting her right index finger in her mouth began to gnaw on the nail.

The tape began scratchily, the French songs came through in a tinny far-off way, but Martin's calm deep commands took over. "Relax, relax . . . look at the light in the ruby chandelier, you're going to sleep . . . No!"

He shut off the tape as he saw her grow limp. "Not *now, Amy* . . . this is only the tape, my dear. I want you to stay awake *now* and tell me *conscious* thoughts. Good Lord, child, you're sure suggestible."

She looked blank.

Martin moved the tape on a bit. "Just listen to what you *did* say and explain it to me, if you can."

She obediently listened, feeling apprehensive and nervous until the tape reached the moment when she had resisted his orders.

As her distorted, sighing voice said, "Wind's will . . ." Martin clicked off the recorder. "What did that mean? Do you know?"

"Of course," she spoke with effort. "It's the—the magic charm to begin the dream. I tried to tell you before. *My Lost Youth* by Longfellow. 'Often I think of the beautiful town that is seated by the sea,' *you* know it, and the ending, 'A boy's will is the wind's

34

will, and the thoughts of youth are long, long thoughts,' but I changed 'boy' to 'girl' in my mind."

"I see," said Martin, suppressing a smile. "When did all this start?"

She frowned. "I guess I was twelve . . . yes, it was eighth grade."

He nodded and switched on the tape. She heard her voice change tone as it rushed into the passionate French sentence, with the high note of fear, or horror, at the end.

"Did I say *that?*" She began to tremble, her pupils darkened.

"Would you translate it, Amy?" he asked gently. "I think I understand what it means, but I want you to translate it." He played her voice back again and waited.

She translated woodenly, though she was still trembling. "It is that I am searching for my love, but the —the fire will—will separate us, l'incendie, what's that in English . . . ?"

"Conflagration," said Martin quietly. "Don't be upset, Amy, I'm trying to help you. Have you ever been in a fire or burned in any way?"

She shook her head.

"Possibly when you were so little you can't remember?"

She shook her head again. "Grandpère would have told me, wouldn't he? No, I know I wasn't. Not *this* me. The *other* Ange-Marie was."

Gosh, Martin thought, dual personality? Well, it happened—there were many books on the subject. Perhaps I *shouldn't* meddle. But, on the other hand— again, he felt a sharp thrust of curiosity, mixed with sympathy.

"Would you like to try this again soon, Amy?" he asked. "We might recover something which would explain your fear of fire. Or would you rather not?"

Her despondent face brightened. "I'd like to try again. Only, the things I said sound so crazy. *Promise* you won't make me go to a psychiatrist."

"I promise," he said slowly. "I don't think you're crazy, and it's not surprising that you talk French under hypnosis since it seems to be your language of the heart, your mother—or rather, father tongue, in this case. How about next Thursday? Same time. And meanwhile, don't think about this session at all, though if you dream, write it down, won't you. . . . Amy—" he added with sudden irritation, "stop looking so—oh, down-trodden, and stop biting your nails! And scuffing your feet! You've shown me other sides of you. Let them out!"

She reddened, her hands dropped, and she stood up straight. To his amused surprise the gray eyes glinted angrily. "I guess I don't want to experiment, Mr. Stone, after all. *Vous êtes trop brusque!*"

Martin laughed outright. "Yes, I *am* too brusk, rude in fact, and I beg your pardon."

As she stood there staring uncertainly at him, he suddenly bent and kissed her lightly on the forehead. "Run along, child, see you in class tomorrow."

Amy walked home in a daze, very conscious of the spot on her forehead where he had kissed her, but also gradually aware that the familiar street did not look right. Those big shiny black-windowed buildings ahead by the railroad station, they shouldn't be there, not all mixed up with trees, elms—luxuriant maples. And on her left, the big motel, the Connecticut Thruway —they were blurring, they grew transparent so that she could see through and way beyond them to the weathered silvery boards of a large water mill and its huge wooden wheel with water dripping off the paddles. She walked on toward the shadowy railroad bridge, while the modern buildings faded. Then, right here on Greenwich Avenue she saw fields studded with the delicate white blossoms of Queen Anne's lace. There were stone walls, too, and a well by a large farmhouse, surrounded by scarlet sumac. At the same time, superimposed like a transparent mirror, she could dimly see the forms of automobiles jammed together, waiting for the light to change.

Behind and through the cars there was a team of plodding white-faced oxen drawing a wagon filled with grain bags, obviously bound for the mill. Past the oxen was a man on horseback, riding up the road which was made of rutted dirt. The man wore a black three-cornered hat and had a high collar and buttons gleaming above his long buff coattails.

Amy gasped, putting her hand out to steady herself on the stone wall. She felt dizzy, but excited.

A blare of horns exploded around her as the traffic light turned green. She squeezed her eyes shut and when she opened them the ox cart and the horseman were respectively transformed into a trailer truck and a large Ford station wagon. The stone wall she was clutching turned into a parking meter. She stared at it stupidly, then snatched her hand away. Electric lights glittered all around her from the shops, the street lamps. Red neons flickered from the movie marquee across the street.

"That was spooky," said Amy aloud, "how nutty can you get?" But still she was more excited than frightened. She was aware of sadness, too, a sense of loss. During that instant when the noise, the crowded bustle, the ugly square buildings had all been transformed, she had also felt the softness of yearning love which came at the beginning of "dreaming true."

Amy looked down at her Mickey Mouse wristwatch, given her by Grandpère for Christmas eight years ago, and still miraculously running. Jeepers! Almost eight o'clock. She hurried up the avenue. The door to their flat was locked and she sighed with relief while she

37

fished out her key. Nobody home yet. She flung her tote bag on the kitchen table and started water boiling for noodles. She had forgotten to eat supper, and anyway, her mother and Grandpère would expect a snack. She did not ponder about her strange experience, which still seemed almost natural.

Back on Steamboat Road Martin paced to and fro for a while, then he picked up the telephone and dialed New York. Claire was home, her voice sounded surprised and pleased. "How you doing with your school kiddies, honey?" she asked. "I was hoping you'd phone some day, nice to hear a voice from home."

Martin and Claire Colbert were both from Louisiana and had dated a few times at Tulane University before he transferred to Duke, then they lost touch with each other, except for an occasional letter and casual glimpses in New Orleans during Christmas vacations.

"Well," said Martin, "too early to tell about my 'kiddies' in general, but I've a kind of problem and I think you're the one to help—if you will."

"Sure will," answered Claire, "ask me out there. This city's driving me bananas, though I like my job when I feel I'm getting some place with my own crazy bunch —at least, *your* pupils are normal, I suppose."

"I'm not so sure," said Martin lightly. "Anyway, can you come out on Sunday? I'll blow you to a good lunch, or if this weather holds, we might picnic."

Claire assented. They arranged trains, and Martin hung up, feeling relieved. The same old frank, humorous, and decisive Claire. He thought about her for a few minutes, her little head with its cap of shining black, carefully groomed elf locks, her highly intelligent blue eyes, the chic way she wore her clothes on a slim, almost boyish body. There had always been a liking between them, but no passion. He vaguely remembered a few kisses on a long-ago night when they drove miles along the levee, but at that age he had been very conscious that she was a class ahead of him in college and was generally considered "a brain"—all very dampening when one was nineteen, but unimportant now. He looked forward to Sunday, and was unaware that he might have indefinitely postponed phoning Claire if it weren't for Amy and his need to talk about her.

The school week finished without incident. Martin ran up to New Haven late on Friday for one of his own advanced classes at Yale. He spent Saturday tidying his home and writing.

On Sunday he met Claire at the Greenwich station and found that they easily picked up their relationship. She had changed little and he was pleased by her well-tailored navy blue pantsuit, her air of tidiness and quiet elegance, and her warmth of greeting. Since the weather was still lovely they decided on a picnic at Greenwich Point and both enjoyed selecting various exotic concoctions from a Chinese restaurant to take with them. They drove to the far end of the Point and settled at a secluded picnic table under the trees. Martin had brought a bottle of dry sherry and some paper cups, from which they toasted each other, smiling.

"This is great," said Claire, loosening her green silk scarf, and lifting her face toward the sunlight as it filtered through maple branches. "Tell me about all the things you never mentioned much in letters, especially that year or so in Vietnam—Saigon—unless you'd rather not."

"I'd rather not," he said, crinkling his eyes, "most of it was pretty painful, until I eventually got clobbered enough to be sent home, then I had an affair with an army nurse, but it didn't last."

"Is *that* your problem?" she asked, smiling a trifle wryly and sipping her sherry. "Some love bind? Though I'm not much qualified to give advice *there*. Except perforce from extensive observation; all the emotionally disturbed teen-agers I try to teach have sex hangups of one kind or another, and none of them gets enough *real* love."

"That's just it," said Martin slowly. "The girl I'm worried about certainly doesn't. Sweet sixteen and never been kissed, I'm sure—believe it or not."

Claire sat up straight. "Martin Stone, you're not cradle-snatching, are you? I shouldn't think you're the type to seduce one of your own students!"

"Of course not!" he responded with heat. "You ought to see the poor kid, she's quite a mess. It's her *psychology* that interests me, there's some very odd things. Here—let's eat and I'll tell you." He opened the boxes of lobster Cantonese, of barbecued spareribs, of rice and sauces, and while they ate he began to talk. Claire listened silently. Her pale oval face showed no expression except once when she raised her eyebrows with a startled look. They finished everything and there was a silence.

"What do you think?" asked Martin at last.

"Extraordinary," said Claire slowly, "and a bit dangerous—your scruples are justified. What are you trying to do? A Bridey Murphy job? Regression to another incarnation?—I don't believe in that stuff, by the way; or like that recent book by Jess Stearn, all those former lives alleged to be uncovered. No, Martin, it won't wash. What's more, if it's a split personality, you *are* dealing with schizophrenia of a kind—or it might be hysteria."

Her positiveness annoyed Martin, who immediately answered more sharply than he meant, "Talk about snap diagnosis! How do you *know*? I'll play you the tape when we get back to my place."

"It won't convince me, I'm afraid," said Claire, "though I do allow such a thing as the collective unconscious, and in this case, possibly some peculiar gene

40

which gives her a pipeline to her own ancestry. Anyway, you present a picture of an unstable, lonely child, for which I'm sorry, but you want my advice, which is —psychiatric counseling, and stop encouraging her fantasy life. Moreover, if you *must* fiddle around with hypnosis, give her constructive suggestions and let it go at that."

Martin swallowed. "You always did lay it on the line, Claire."

She saw the annoyance in his hazel eyes and sighed. "Another thing," she said softly, "please don't start thinking of yourself as Pygmalion—or Professor Higgins in *My Fair Lady,* or you'll get involved even more than you are now."

Martin frowned, pushing together all the little empty cartons, then lighting his pipe. He knew that Claire might be right in her reactions, and yet . . .

"Did it ever occur to you that I might *help* Amy, just by being her friend? And that if I could uncover what *really* frightens her, let her explore those peculiar dreams of hers, that besides growing up to be a whole woman, there could be a great break-through in the mysterious realms of the mind. Good Lord, Claire, you've a Ph.D., has that made you academic and hide bound?"

Claire watched a squirrel go chittering up a tree for a moment. She fished a cigarette out of her green leather handbag and lit it.

"I think not," she said carefully. "Martin, you asked my advice and I gave it, but I don't want us to quarrel." She hesitated, and looking sternly at the squirrel, added in a low voice, "I don't believe in fuzzy crackpot experiments with the psyche. Leave it at that. But I personally don't want this to be our last reunion. Do you?" She rose, and sweeping up all the picnic trash, carried it to a garbage can.

Martin answered her question when she came back.

"No, I don't want us to quarrel, my dear, all the same, I'm going on with my experiment. Let's talk of something else. Tell me about your life. Lovers? Wining and dining? You said you hated the city, but there's a lot to do there."

Claire powdered her delicate tip-tilted nose and applied a touch of irridescent pink lipstick before she shrugged and said, "No lovers at present. Oh, I date now and then, one Charles in particular." She hesitated. "I'm not sure about Charles yet—but I haven't found a Yankee I really like much. They're in such a hurry. Then you might say I'm wedded to my job, which pays very well, by the way. My special school is select—rich parents. But I work nights sometimes, as a volunteer in Harlem."

"You would," said Martin, smiling and trying to lighten their disagreement. "Dedicated type, though you don't look it, actually. I like the way you dress, and that sexy perfume, what is it?" He was still attracted to her and yet he found her attitude irritating. He had hoped she would co-operate in his researches, perhaps ask to meet Amy, which would lead apparently, he now realized, to precisely the psychiatric inquisition the girl feared.

"The perfume is Yardley's lavender soap, I suppose," said Claire with a small laugh. "You always were a romantic at heart, moonlight and magnolias. You were conditioned to all that on 'the old plantation,' and by your beautiful, doting mother. I saw her once at a Comus Ball. But *I* grew up, remember, in a perfectly ordinary apartment in the *un*glamorous part of New Orleans, and my father was a mere overworked doctor, a general practitioner, while *my* mother, who was German, firmly disciplined her brood and doubled as office nurse for Father. No languorous Creole blood in *me*, Martin." She made a brisk gesture with her hand.

"So I see," he said, laughing, though he was piqued, and she knew it. "Well, do you want to decide on a train, or shall we go back to my apartment and listen to the stereo. I've got some new albums."

He added the last invitation because of inbred courtesy, though a stilted antagonism had arisen between them. In the beginning when she arrived, Martin had wanted to kiss her—perhaps more. Now he did not.

"I've decided on a train," said Claire. "I've got a time table. Must work tonight, mountains of papers."

He acceded at once and they chatted casually on the platform until the train drew in.

Just as she said, "Good-by and thanks," her face tightened. "I'm sorry, Martin, that we can't agree on your problem. I simply think you're heading for trouble. I'm sorry. . . ." she repeated in a stifled voice and boarded the train.

Martin went home in a very bad humor.

On the following Thursday night Martin received Amy with a cordiality which was born partly from his conflict with Claire. He noted that Amy had let her hair fall loose on her shoulders, and that expectation gave a sparkle to her face.

She sat down with a little sound of contentment as she looked around his living room, at the view of the harbor, the books, the ruby chandelier.

"I haven't been dreaming," she said, earnestly reporting, "not exactly, but other funny things have happened."

"Oh . . . .?" he said, "like what?"

She told him of the strange moment upon leaving his flat last week when she had seen a water mill, oxen, farmhouses, and a horseman, all seeming more real than Greenwich Avenue's normal scene.

Martin was dismayed and fascinated. "Anything like

that ever happen before while you were awake?" he asked, frowning.

"No, but it seemed natural somehow. I wasn't frightened."

Martin crossed his legs, puffed on his pipe a moment, then said, "I think you trust me, and I believe you're truthful, Amy. There's plenty of pot-smoking in your age group, we know, some hard drugs, too, alas. Have you ever taken anything?"

Amy shook her head. "Jeb wanted me to try pot once —that's Jeb Jones. I took a few whiffs and choked. I didn't like it. As for the hard stuff, maybe *some* do, but I wouldn't know. I don't really have any friends." She sighed. "I don't know how to make friends and Mother doesn't like me to bring anyone home."

Martin was touched and totally convinced. In her own way Amy was as frank as Claire. "Well, *I'm* your friend, Amy," he said with more warmth than he meant to show. He hastily motioned to the tape recorder on the table. "Shall we try this again now?"

"Sure," she said, looking at him with a yielding softness. Martin hastily began the routine speeches. Very soon she relaxed, then she shut her eyes at his command.

"Very good," said Martin, switching on the tape. "First listen—'A girl's will is the wind's will, and the thoughts of youth are long long thoughts'—do you see anything, Amy?"

She nodded, her face changed in the subtle way it had before, it became rosier, the mouth seemed fuller, while the lips curved in a sweetly provocative smile.

"Where are you, Amy?" he asked quietly.

"*Grand Pré dans l'Acadie,*" she answered.

"And *who* are you?" he pursued.

"*Ange-Marie. J'ai quinze ans. Je viens du boulanger qui est mon père. Je me promène dans la grande route, mes sabots font claque-claque sur le pavé, je*

44

*suis heureuse parce que Paul m'attend dans la chau-
mière des Delatours."*

Martin swallowed, thrilled with her responses, yet
not entirely certain of their meaning. Her French was
peculiar, the stresses alien to him. This is going to be
a stumbling block, he thought. A bad one, unless . . .
He leaned forward intently.

"Have you a long story to tell, Ange-Marie?"

"Ouais, historie mainte longue et fort tragique."

"Since you understand my English questions, I
want you to answer in English," he said, holding his
breath. "You know English perfectly *now,* perhaps you
even learned it *then.*"

Her little face contorted, its mouth drooped sullenly.
"I hate the English," she said. "The new English, too.
Both very harsh, very bad. We try to keep peace, but
they hate *us,* cruelty, exile, b-burnings."

He saw that she was upset, her body was trembling
again, her hands clenching together, and Martin deemed
it wise to check her, though he was triumphant that she
had answered him in English.

"Quiet, child—" he said in a soothing voice. "Stop
thinking of bad times. Can you remember some happy ones?"

The anger gradually dissolved from her face, "Happy with Paul," she said in a voice of great sweetness.
"We loved—we made love on the beach of the long
island, an hour's walk from Grand Pré. Blomidon
loomed dark across the Beau Bassin. Yes, we built a
little play hut together on the sand out of pine
boughs, but one day the great tide came, bigger tide
than usual even, it crept up while we were making love
and wet us. It was funny!" The girl chuckled. "We
laughed so much."

But this sounds *true,* Martin thought, while his heart
beat fast. "What year did all this happen, Ange-Marie?
Do you know?"

She hesitated a minute, *"Dix-sept cent cinquante-cinq,"* she responded slowly, *"avant le Grand Dérangement."*

"In English, please."

She bit her lips and was silent for a minute, then she obeyed. "Seventeen fifty-five, before the—the—" she gulped, putting her hands to her face.

"All right, dear, all right—" said Martin, "now you're going to wake up. I'll count slowly from one to ten, then I'll tap the table and you'll wake up. One ... two ... three ..."

When he had rapped sharply on the table she opened her eyes and stared at him in a dazed way. "When do we start?" she said. "I thought you were going to hypnotize me."

"I guess I *did,"* Martin laughed ruefully. He could hear Claire's scorn. "What sort of evidence is it that you got? Nothing the girl might not have read, heard from her grandfather, or imagined."

"Amy," he said, "how much do you know about the expulsion of the French Acadians from Nova Scotia in 1755? I know that your own ancestors were among the exiles, you told me so."

"Why—" said Amy, "I guess I know the general facts, and then from Grandpère, and Longfellow who invented Evangeline Bell-fontaine, and made her so pathetic and deeply faithful. Anyway, it's all a muddle and it was really Ange-Marie who suffered."

"Oh, it was, was it?" said Martin thoughtfully. "You mean your ancestress?"

Amy nodded.

"And did she marry?"

"Yes, somebody called Delatour, but there's a mystery about him. Grandpère doesn't know what happened, except a Delatour came back to Nova Scotia, a different part from Grand Pré, the west coast—that's why Grandpère was born there."

46

"H-mmm," said Martin. "Have you ever heard that Ange-Marie's husband might have been called Paul?"

"No," said Amy. "Grandpère doesn't know his name. Mr. Stone, I have a kind of headache. I'm sorry. I think I ought to get back."

"Yes, of course," he was apologetic and also impressed by her sudden maturity. "I get carried away, I'm afraid. Thank you for coming. Are you sure you can get home OK?"

She nodded, but did not answer. After she left he realized that she had not asked to hear the tape, nor perhaps understood that there was anything to hear.

Martin went to the public library the following afternoon, and spent two hours researching the Acadians. He also found a map showing the Nova Scotia region around Grand Pré which Amy had twice mentioned during the trance. He discovered that there *was* a Long Island with a beach, referred to on the modern map as "Evangeline's" beach. And that across the bay with its Fundy tides—the highest in the world—there was a high cape called Blomidon. Still, he told himself, all this was nothing which would impress Claire.

Even though Amy denied special knowledge, or any travel except to Massachusetts for Longfellow, she *had,* by her own admission, spent much time in libraries, she might even have found out these geographical facts.

Next, Martin turned to Greenwich history. How valid was Amy's peculiar vision on Greenwich Avenue?

From the few available books on old-time Greenwich, he discovered that there was indeed a mill on Horseneck Brook, just where it emptied into the Sound at the harbor, and that Greenwich Avenue *had* been a winding dirt road throughout the eighteenth century, and there had been a Mead farmhouse, located nearly opposite the present movie theater. *Mead,* he thought, that's odd—has she some atavistic relationship to her mother's side, too? Though his source books showed that there were then hundreds of Meads in the township.

Perhaps Amy had also read Greenwich books. Claire would certainly say so, and furthermore, she would say that if the girl was beginning to hallucinate in her waking moments, then she must reiterate her remark as she boarded the train . . . "I think you're heading for trouble."

Damn Claire, he thought, with a spurt of entirely masculine rage. Martin came from a family whose women were decorative, gentle, and never aspired to knowledge superior to that of their men. And I'll handle this fascinating case myself, without harming Amy.

Chapter Three

The next days slid by without any special communication between Martin and Amy. She appeared in his Chaucer class, asked an occasional intelligent question, which showed that she had—naturally in view of her background—far less trouble than the others in understanding Chaucer's fourteenth-century mixture of French-English, but their contact was limited to the classroom.

Martin noted that Amy's reddish brown hair had a pretty sheen as it now curled loosely below her shoulders, and that she twice wore a simple little cotton dress which revealed that she must have lost weight and that her figure was not nearly as shapeless as he had thought.

But he decided not to single her out in any way and was doubtful about their Thursday night date, since he could not entirely ignore Claire's advice.

Amy had no doubts at all. She no longer felt friendless, life had more purpose, and on a far deeper level than the stage in which she had been so obsessed with Longfellow. She felt new growth stirring deep within her, like the first green tendrils pushing through heavy spring soil. She had ceased to dream, and yet, another peculiar thing happened to her.

On that Friday a group of juniors from the high school had been taken on a field trip to an old house in Cos Cob, which was the headquarters of the Greenwich Historical Society, and Amy, impulsively, on the Monday following in the girls' locker room, had asked about the trip.

"Oh, it was neat, real interesting," said Judy somebody, pleased to be questioned by a senior. "It's a terribly old house, they've got a fantastic cellar and a spooky attic. And I didn't know there were ever black slaves in *Greenwich!* But they showed us the quarters and said the Bushes—that was the family then—had a lot of them."

"I didn't know either," said Amy, clutching a towel around her middle as she walked into the shower.

These chance remarks impressed Amy. They gave her a sudden thrill, half afraid, yet compulsive.

On Tuesday after school she hesitated a while outside the building, absently watching the cheerleaders practicing their football routine. These girls were all picked for their looks and verve; Doris Drake was, of course, among them. Doris in her sweater and pleated skirt, with golden hair flying beneath a red band as she leapt and twirled—well, you couldn't miss Doris, nor the knot of football players who gathered admiringly around her. Amy's familiar pang of envy was somewhat muted today. She had decided on an expedition.

She told herself that it would be a lovely surprise for Grandpère if she went to visit him in his tiny woodworking shop, especially as inquiry had elicited the fact that the old Bush-Holley House in Cos Cob was quite near to him and she wanted to visit it. Wanted to badly enough to have saved some lunch money and withheld a dollar from Sunday evening's baby sitting. Her mother grumbled and Amy had been uncharacteristically stubborn. "I've a right to *some* allowance, Mother. Jeepers, I haven't even been to a movie in—in ages." And that was six months ago when she had sneaked out with Jeb, she thought. "I'll do extra hours for the Robinsons next Saturday to make up, though their four-year-old is the brattiest kid I've ever had to sit for. He up-chucks his supper every time, then giggles like mad while I clean up the mess."

"Beggars can't be choosers," said Sarah glumly. "What do you want the dollar for? I buy you everything you need, and it'll have to be snow boots next, I suppose. Your feet get bigger and bigger."

"No," said Amy, "I think I've quit growing. The old boots'll do—if we have another mild winter."

Sarah frowned uncertainly at her child, the indifferent calm reply baffled her. Amy was changing somehow, "escaping" was almost the word which came into Sarah's unhappy mind. She was not quite aware that she preferred the old indifferent obedient Amy, that uncomfortable as their life was, and jealous as she was of the affection between her daughter and the grandfather, still there *had* been a structure about it.

She tried to regain her weakening authority with a half concession. "Well, so long as you pay back the dollar—but, Amy, why've you taken to letting your hair go frowzy, you always kept it neat, as any self-respecting girl should. You trying to ape those little minxes at the school?"

Amy put up her hands and smoothed the long strands of gleaming hair. "I'm not trying to ape anybody, Mother," she said, "but I know it's prettier this way . . . you don't *want* me to try and be pretty, do you!"

Sarah flushed. She slowly straightened her aching back. "Handsome is as handsome does," she snapped, using a tag from her own unloved orphaned childhood. She added unwillingly, so low that Amy could hardly hear her, "You're getting more and more like your father. . . ." She seized a dishrag and began cleaning the already spotless sink. I'd guess there was some boy she's after, Sarah thought bitterly, except I know none's been after *her,* without you count that no-good colored boy—it can't be a *boy* making her change, and she's so young, sixteen's hardly more than a child.

Amy looked at her mother's bent back, at the slight tremor in the gnarled hands, the peevish sharp-drawn face, and for a second felt pity, or at least a quiver of understanding. She touched Sarah's bony arm gently and Sarah winced away. She detested physical contact. Amy sighed and slipped out the door.

She boarded a commercial bus bound toward Stamford. It stopped in Cos Cob. Amy descended and walked along the River Road until she saw her grandfather's modest sign, P. DELATOUR, CABINET-MAKING & WOODWORK. The shop was nothing but a shack, huddled between other ramshackle buildings near the marina. It was heated only by an old pot-bellied stove, into which he fed wood shavings, and lit when necessary by one dangling electric bulb.

The old man was planing a board as she pushed open the door and he turned around eagerly. *"Ah, ma chérie,"* he said, at once forgetting disappointment that she was not a customer. He put down the plane and gave her a bear hug. "So you want to see what your old Grandpère is up to? I am enchanted by your visit."

Amy kissed him. "Is that the dog kennel?" she asked, also in French. She walked to an elaborately carved little house made of oak, with the name NERO above the door. She ran her fingers over the curlicues and wooden ornamentations. "That Mrs. Riston must be thrilled. I'm sure she'll give you other work."

"One may hope so," he said, sighing. "She said she'd send her station wagon for it this morning, but it hasn't come yet."

"Oh well, then later, or tomorrow," said Amy confidently, though her heart misgave her. He looked tired and worried, but he had had no more frightening attacks. She felt guilty because it was not really to see her grandfather that she had come to Cos Cob.

"I've a—an errand," she said, "but I'll be back this way and we'll catch the home bus together, shall we?"

He assented without question. Grandpère never probed, but his keen dark eyes looked at her with sudden attention between the wrinkled lids.

"Ange-Marie . . ." he said, "you look different today, or is it the light through these dusty windows?" He gestured with his veined hand, "You resemble . . . ah . . . what can it be . . . ?" He frowned, trying to recapture a likeness which went back and back in memory to his childhood in Nova Scotia. A little painted picture—a miniature of a girl with dark hair, wide eyes, and a sweetly smiling mouth, on her head a white cap with wings. A wedding picture, treasured in the Delatour family, and long since disappeared. Who was it of? Some ancestress, he could not remember which. He shrugged.

"I'm getting old . . ." he said, sighing again, then smiling. "I begin to live in the past. Trot along on your errand."

Amy walked out on the River Road toward a bridge over the mill pond, while her grandfather's words echoed in her mind. *"Le Passé."* The past. Time that has gone forever. But has it? Was it that simple? She had never flown, but she could easily imagine how it would be in an airplane. The expanded view for hundreds of miles down below. Those cars moving on the Thruway, she glanced at the actual Connecticut Turnpike, which roared by high on a trestle over the cove. In those cars they couldn't see anything right now but the bridge over the cove, but from an airplane one could see where one had been two hours ago and where one was going. It would all seem to be happening at the same *time* in space. Except that she herself wouldn't much want to see where they were *going,* that was subtly distasteful, she would look at where they had been—New York? New Jersey? even Washington! Or in the west-bound lane from Hartford—Boston, maybe Canada? Or could one see as far away as Canada? She did not know, but she felt an odd sensation steal over her. A breathless anticipation, a tingling. She stood on the bridge in the gathering twilight and looked ahead at the buff-colored house with white porches, rearing up behind a tall stone wall.

Ah yes, she thought, *that's* the house, but it didn't used to have porches and it used to be red instead of tan. I've stood here before on the bridge, except then it was narrow and wooden. I was scared. I didn't know if they'd take me in, though I had a permit in my skirt pocket. I was very tired, my feet hurt—walking, walking—I had a bundle on my back, everything I owned. I was unhappy. I couldn't find Paul—all those weeks, no, months, almost a year—since the exile—and the angry Yankees who wouldn't speak French. *Did* they *kill* Paul?

Amy shuddered and jumped back as a delivery truck honked behind her. While it passed the strange unhappy feeling vanished. She walked with determination toward the old house and saw a small sign swinging from a post, BUSH-HOLLEY HOUSE.

She crossed Strickland Road and mounted several stone steps, then some wooden ones onto the porch. She rang a bell at the most likely door. It was opened by a middle-aged woman with a pleasant face.

"Can I see the house?" Amy asked, and her voice quivered.

"Well, I guess so," said the guide, looking surprised. "It's almost closing time."

"I want to *so* much. I missed out when the high school juniors came, Friday, but they said it was neat."

The guide smiled. "All right, if you're a student," she said. "Now we'll start in the little counting room, to the left here . . . the wallpaper is very old, about 1750 . . . it has tax stamps from George the II of England."

Amy scarcely listened. She was absorbed in a sense of familiarity combined with a feeling that she must find a certain place upstairs, but she said nothing and obediently followed the guide.

She duly admired the lovely paneling in the parlor, and the beehive oven in the long room; upstairs there was more paneling in a bedroom. She peered up into the old garret with its massive chimney, she went through several small rooms, some given over to exhibitions. She hesitated in one which contained many books and was called the "library," but in none did she find exactly the place she was half-consciously seeking.

"What's down that way?" Amy finally asked, pointing to a door by the entrance to the west wing, as the guide started to descend the stairs.

"Oh, that was the slave quarters. The curator has a room at the end which is private."

"Yes," said Amy, nodding with a flash of certainty. "That's where the slaves slept—Jupiter, Phillis, and poor little Candy." Amy broke off as she saw the guide staring at her. "I mean, one of the girls from Friday *told* me there were slaves. I was surprised."

The guide nodded, perplexed. She, like Pierre Delatour earlier, found an eeriness in Amy's earnest bespectacled face, something strange in the breathless certainty of the voice. "There *were* slaves of such names," the guide said, "we have the records, I guess you must have read the official pamphlet? In fact, there were eleven slaves in 1797, judging from the Bush inventory."

Not eleven when I was here, Amy thought. They only had three, and I slept on a trundle bed with Candy. She had wandered into the cluttered room which housed glass exhibition cases. She went to a corner at the west end by a window. The guide followed uneasily and switched on the lights, for it was growing dark.

"The books in this case were all written here or pertain to the house in its days as the Holley Inn," she said automatically, but she was growing more uncomfortable, for the girl ignored the glass case and stared fixedly at one spot. "Come along, I'm afraid it's closing time."

"There was an outside staircase, right where that low window is," said Amy, pointing to the north wall. "Phillis got stuck on it once, she was so fat and clumsy. She was pregnant, too."

The guide swallowed. There had always been suspicion of an outside staircase, but none of the reconstruction architects was certain . . . the rest of the girl's speech . . . well. . . . "Come, dear," she said, trying to keep her voice steady and persuasive. "We must go down. Do you live far? How are you going to get home?"

The clinging mists dissolved in Amy's mind. She blinked. "Oh, of course," she said, "I'm sorry to keep you. I'm going home with my grandfather, he's waiting on the River Road. But isn't there a little wash house near the garden?"

The guide nodded and said sharply, "Too late to see the exhibits there tonight, or the barn. You can come back on a school tour." When, thank heaven, I won't

56

be alone with her, the guide thought. The girl may be emotionally disturbed . . . wonder if I ought to report it. But as Amy made polite farewells and docilely went downstairs the guide decided that the incident was trivial. There had been other peculiar people among the hordes who came to see the house. She forgot Amy as she saw her out, then locked up and hurried home through the little kitchen door to her dinner. She would not have been so easily reassured had she seen Amy leaning against the front stone wall, sobbing quietly, before turning and walking over the bridge, back to Grandpère's shop.

After all, Martin decided not to cancel out his rendezvous with Amy just yet, and on Thursday it had turned cool, at last.

When Amy presented herself at Martin's flat he ushered her into a living room made cosy and welcoming by a wood fire burning on his hearth. Amy took one frightened look at the fire and shrank back to the entrance. "I can't stay," she said, clutching the door knob. "Not with *that* here."

She had actually yanked the front door open again before he grabbed her arm and pulled her back into the room. "Good Lord, Amy, don't be ridiculous! There's nothing to be frightened of."

He felt her tremble and saw her face go very white. "I want to get away," she whispered, pushing at him and shutting her eyes.

Martin was astounded. Bad as that . . . he thought . . . they were right when they mentioned pyrophobia. "Look, my dear, this fire gives us beauty and warmth. I think it's lovely and so must you."

She shook her head violently. "I can't stay. I hate it, it burned . . . burned up . . ." Her terror was so obvious that he gave in.

"I'll put it out, come with me to the kitchen, help me get water."

She went with him, dragging her steps, and she would not leave the kitchen while he brought a kettle and reluctantly doused his hearth fire. As the smoking embers blackened and hissed, he put the screen in front of them and led her back into the living room. "Now what *is* all this, Amy? You must have seen open fires before."

She shook her head. "No, and it took me years to be able to light the gas burners; I still grit my teeth when I do."

"Hmm," said Martin. He remembered various phobias of which he'd read. Fear of heights, fear of cats, he'd had an aunt with *that* one, and claustrophobia—the commonest of all. But there must be some reason, some buried trauma to explain. Amy denied all memory of dangerous fires during her short years of living, but . . . if there *could* have been another life . . . Never mind, skip it for now . . .

Amy had relaxed and was sitting in her usual seat, her head still averted from the dead embers.

"Anything new this week," he asked in a light tone, "dreams, maybe?"

"No, not exactly. But . . . in a way . . . not *dream* . . . it was when I went to the Bush-Holley House, you know, the Historical Society place in Cos Cob?"

"Yes," said Martin. He had arrived in Greenwich a couple of weeks before the opening of school to give himself time to settle in and to arrange his courses at Yale. And being of a curious nature had taken time to investigate such sights as Greenwich could offer. Bred as he was to spacious plantation homes and "garden tours," which always included his own magnificent columned birthplace Bellerive, on the Bayou Teche, he had not been much impressed by old New England architecture.

"Yes," repeated Martin, "I've been there—why?"

"Because," said Amy, "I went to see it Tuesday. Something made me. It was queer . . ." She bit her lips and stared past his head toward the window and the waters of Greenwich Harbor.

"What was queer? The house?"

"Not exactly—the way I felt. I *knew* that house, parts of it. I *knew* where I'd slept then with . . . with Candy. I could feel her warm brown little body snuggled against mine in the cold nights. I could hear her crying, she cried a lot, but it was worse later when they shut her up in the wash house—and she died there." Amy caught her breath.

Oh, Lord, Martin thought, *now* what! And yet Amy's unemphatic sad voice was convincing, though he tried to combat the impression with a smile, saying, "My dear girl, you have a powerful imagination. I'll bet you grow up into a writer—poetry maybe. Have you tried any?"

She brushed this off impatiently. "I keep telling you these things were . . . *are* real. They *happened*. I can *remember*. Candy was burning with fever, she had a terrible earache. That's why she cried so much. They thought she was faking because she wouldn't do the laundry, just kept moaning. That's why they locked her in the wash house, to make her work."

"*Who* did?" asked Martin sharply.

"Mistress Bush," Amy answered. "The first one. But the slaves Jupiter and Phillis *helped* punish Candy. They couldn't stand her crying either, and she wasn't *their* child. The day after they shut her up Candy gave an awful scream and must have died right after. When we found her she had pus and blood running out of her ear. Something had burst."

That sounds remarkably like mastoiditis, Martin thought. And it also sounds remarkably circumstantial. He was silent a moment. "What do you think *you* were doing at that house? And why were you sleeping with the slaves?" he asked quietly.

Amy looked troubled. "I'm not sure, except that they didn't want me . . . the Bushes, I was quartered on them by the . . . the . . . government. They didn't like me because I only spoke French and was a Catholic and I cried a lot, too. You see, I couldn't find Paul. We were all scattered and I didn't have anyone with me. I think my father was sent to prison in England, and Mother . . . she died on the ship coming down here. I don't know where my brothers went, maybe they finally got to Louisiana to the Cajun country. I don't know."

Could this possibly be true? Martin thought. She is seeing herself as one of the exiled Acadians, she knows much of their story, but none ever came to *Greenwich!* That's fantastic.

He looked at the girl with keen attention, her eyes were unfocussed, she was lying back limp in her chair, her hands fallen open. "I heard Candy's ghost crying from the wash house again on Tuesday," she whispered.

"Amy!" he cried, "are you awake? Sit up and answer me."

She did so slowly. "I guess I'm awake. You didn't put me to sleep, did you? Have I been saying silly things?"

"Not exactly," said Martin, "but I don't understand them. And I did *not* hypnotize you. I think you hypnotized yourself. Look here, Amy, I'm out of my depth. I don't think you better come here any more. Aside from the way the school would react if they knew of these visits, I blame myself for starting this. And I'm afraid it isn't doing you any good."

"Oh, it *is!* It *is!*" she cried in a quivering voice. "You can't stop now. I'd be too unhappy. I was be-

60

fore, but I didn't know it. You've *got* to help me, Mr. Stone."

Martin was silent, dismayed by her desperation, and suffering strong pangs of guilt.

"I don't want to be arbitrary . . ." he said, reluctantly, at last, "but I don't know that it's wise to let you churn up the past . . . whatever it was, or you imagine it was, I want you to face realities right now."

Amy sighed with relief, sensing his capitulation. She gave him a small wistful smile. "I *don't* exactly imagine," she said. "At least the other thing keeps bugging me. It's all inside me and wants to get out. The other Ange-Marie wants to get out."

Martin crossed his legs and drew on his pipe. And what would Claire think of that remark! Definitely psychotic. Confusion. I should break my promise and send Amy to the clinic . . . or one of the many psychiatrists in town . . . but not yet.

"Well . . ." he said slowly, "shall we try straight hypnosis once more, and speak to me in English, Amy—I would like to find out why you're so afraid of fire, there's got to be something in your infancy you've blocked out. So lie back and look up at the light in the chandelier until you get sleepy." He unobtrusively turned on the tape and began the soothing monotonous commands.

Very soon she went limp again and her eyelids dropped.

"Where are you, Amy? What do you see?" he asked quietly.

She answered at once in a whisper, *"Je suis sur le bateau, je vois le village de Gaspereau, et l'incendie . . ."*

"In *English*," he commanded. She swallowed, seeming to make an effort. "I am on the ship with my poor mother. We see the village of Gaspereau, all

61

in flames. Our new house, too, and behind, against the darkness of Cap Blomidon, the village of Grand Pré is burning. I haven't seen Paul since they locked him in the church with the other men. Nor my father and brothers. Those English, they wrenched us away, they threw us like beasts in the ship . . . many ships . . . we were separated. As our ship sailed out of the harbor we could see everything we loved, our houses, our crops, even the church we were so proud of, all in flames." She stopped, a spasm contorted her face.

"Is that it, Ange-Marie?" he asked gently. "Were those the flames which make you so afraid?"

"No," she said, to his surprise, "other ones, later. When I . . . I couldn't . . ." She began to shiver, then tremble so hard that Martin cut in sharply, "Never mind. Forget all that, whatever it was. Think of Paul. Were you scared for *him?*"

She stopped trembling, she even smiled a little. "Oh no, for I prayed Paul would be all right. Would escape somehow. He had Indian friends in the forest. Mishadoga—that was his friend. But I hadn't seen Paul since they imprisoned him and the others in the church. I didn't know where he went. He didn't know where *I* was. We searched . . . searched so long . . . the endless years, and then in the end . . ." She began to cry, tears running down beneath her closed lids.

"OK, Amy," said Martin. "That's enough. I want you to wake up now, when I've finished counting. You will feel happy and be happy tomorrow. You'll sleep well tonight and be refreshed."

He counted slowly, then rapped on the table, fearing that she might not obey him—the fear, he knew, of every hypnotist.

But she opened her eyes, giving a rending yawn. "What did I say?" she asked eagerly.

"Nothing important," answered Martin. "I don't think we'll go into it. But how do you feel?"

"OK," she said. "Sort of sleepy, though I guess I'll go home and tackle Longfellow again. But I'm awfully slow at it. I've kind of lost touch with him."

She pulled a pink lipstick from her purse and applied it clumsily. "Mother doesn't like me to use *any* make-up," she said, "but I think I look better with some, don't you?"

Martin did. He was also aware of several changes in the girl during the last weeks. Natural, perhaps, at sixteen. "Standing with reluctant feet, where the brook and river meet, womanhood and childhood fleet"—that blasted Longfellow, one *did* remember tags from his poems. Amy's infected me, he thought wryly, even though she is losing interest in him, since he seems to have provided only the key to unlock her bizarre interior life. And it sure was bizarre. All that rigmarole about the Bush-Holley House simply did not fit.

He glanced at his wristwatch. "Lord, it's almost nine. I better run you home in my car. We don't," he added with a smile, "want you hallucinating on Greenwich Avenue again, and I'm sure you don't want to tell unnecessary lies to your mother and grandfather." And I, he thought, don't want a fuss. A teacher had been fired last year for what the high school considered irregular behavior with a student.

"Grandpère would never question me," said Amy, "and Mother's bus doesn't get in for an hour, but I'd like to ride, if you want to. I'll do anything you want, except *please* don't say I can't come here . . . or do you think I'm a nuisance?" She lifted her chin in the proud little gesture which always took him by surprise. It seemed so unlike her usual docility, and from the "dowdy mouse" concept he had first formed of her. His innate gallantry swamped his better judgment and made him give her reassurance.

"Not a nuisance, of course, and we won't decide anything final about another visit right now. I've got an errand in town anyway, so come on."

He drove swiftly up Arch Street so as to come down the oneway avenue and deposit her at her door. He was uneasily conscious that she was snuggling against him and that he enjoyed the contact, until he felt her jump, stiffen, and heard her say, "Damn and spit!" under her breath, while he drew into a parking space quite near the deli.

"Really, Amy," he said laughing, then he saw what she had seen. A tall, gaunt woman in a shabby brown coat standing under the street light.

"It's Mother," said Amy, "and she's seen us."

Sarah walked up to the Volkswagen. "And where have you been, Miss—and who's that?" She pointed at Martin. He got out as Amy did and addressed the scowling Sarah. "I'm Martin Stone, Mrs. Delatour, Amy's English teacher, I live just down there on Steamboat Road. I've been giving her extra help with her independent study project." His southern drawl was at its most pronounced, his manner extremely courteous. This was not his first encounter with suspicious mothers.

"At this time of night?" shrilled Sarah, "and where, I'd like to know!"

Martin disliked lies, but there was a season for everything and he could feel Amy's fear. "I hold evening seminars from time to time in my home," he said. "Amy is almost the brightest student in the senior class, Mrs. Delatour, are you aware of that? She deserves every encouragement."

Sarah was nonplussed. This tall, assured young man and her daughter, who was looking at her with growing defiance—though she could hardly see any

64

expressions by the street light—they both daunted her. The ache in her back which had forced her to leave the store early, sent an excruciating twinge down her right leg.

"Well . . ." she said, frowning, "there wasn't any goings on like this when I went to school, though I suppose if Amy can get through school fast . . . earn some real wages some place . . ."

"Amy is college material, Mrs. Delatour," said Martin coldly. "She should be applying now."

"Don't call me *that!*" Sarah's miseries and baffled anger suddenly focused on his pronunciation of her name. "It's *Delay*ter, as you should know, unless Amy's up to tricks like her no-good father." She glared at the girl. "What've you done with your glasses? You're blind as a mole without 'em."

"Not quite, Mother." Having recovered from her initial panic, Amy spoke in the new, faintly scornful voice. "Don't you think we should ask Mr. Stone upstairs for a cup of coffee, since he's been so kind to me? I'd like him to meet Grandpère."

Sarah tried to refuse. She hated folk to see how they lived, all cramped together and no decent parlor, no place to sit except the kitchen, and Mr. Delayter's dirty supper dishes piled in the sink, likely as not, since Amy hadn't been home to do them, but her leg gave another twinge and she turned silently toward the entrance steps in ungracious assent.

Martin followed the woman and the girl upstairs. He did not want to, yet he was curious to meet her grandfather, nor could he let Amy down in what he perceived to be a small victory.

Pierre Delatour came out of his bedroom when he heard voices and greeted Martin with a startled and then hearty welcome, which slipped from English into French, as usual when he was excited. He missed visitors very much and endured this unnatural isolation only because of Amy. She alone prevented him from going back to his country, to Rivière du Loup, where some of his old friends were still living. He could have had a room with the Gautiers, where there would be good hearty food, hard cider, gossip, and one could smoke the clay pipe whenever one wished. An annual Christmas card assured him of his welcome, but he had managed to conceal from Amy the longings and the sadness he often felt.

Now here was Amy with a suitable young man at last, and his daughter-in-law looking as though she had sucked pickles, while she sniffed in her unpleasant way and announced, "I'm going to retire. I guess you won't stay long, Mr. . . . Mr. . . . Stone." She disappeared but left her bedroom door open a crack, as propriety demanded.

Amy went to the stove to start coffee; Martin seated himself at the center table next to the old man, whose bearded face was beaming as he plied Martin with questions. So he was a teacher? And he came from Louisiana, and did he know the Bayou Teche way off in the western part of the state? Ah . . . then he must have met some Cajuns?

"I believe I 'ad an ancester went zere," said Pierre. "Oh, long way back . . . *longtemps,* just after *le Grand Dérangement,* 'e go to La Louisiane. But 'e get *mal du pays* . . . 'ow you say in English?"

"Homesickness," said Amy softly, setting a cup of instant coffee before Martin. She continued, smiling, "And he came back to Canada, didn't he, Grandpère? And brought his son." She had heard the story many times. "He couldn't go really *home* to Grand Pré because the English moved in and rebuilt some of the burned houses for themselves. So he went to St. Mary's Bay on the western shore of Nova Scotia, where there were other Acadian refugees."

Martin looked at her, then at the old man. "What was this ancestor's name, do you know?"

Pierre shrugged and smiled. "Delatour . . . *évidemment, monsieur* . . . since I am a direct descendant."

"Yes, but his first name, his Christian name?"

"Zat I don't remember, mebbe Louis or Pierre, like mine. Was so long ago nobody could write down in zose days. But zere was always une Ange-Marie in ze family—like now." He patted Amy's hand as she poured hot milk into his coffee. She responded by brushing her cheek against his thick grizzled hair, gestures of affection which touched Martin, who liked the old man as much as he disliked the mother.

"Could you, *monsieur,* per'aps come to my shop one day?" asked Delatour eagerly. "I'd like show you my *ménuiserie,* we could smoke together . . . *hein?*" He had noticed the stem of Martin's pipe in the breast pocket, he glanced toward Sarah's door and lowered his voice. "Tak' a leetle glass together, I've cognac saved, very old, from when my son was living, or if you like music, I sing you Canadian songs. *'Allouette, gentille allouette,'*" he burst out in a powerful baritone, quite carried away with this tiny social occasion.

"*Je te plumerai le bec. Je te plumerai le bec—et le bec, et le bec—O—O—hh, Allouette, gentille allouette. . . .*" He thumped the table with gusto, remembering his youth.

Martin understood the measure of the man's loneliness, and also of Amy's, when there was a sharp command from Sarah's bedroom.

"Mr. Delayter, stop that awful caterwauling!"

"I'll visit your shop, sir," said Martin hastily. "Be charmed to. But I must go now."

Pierre Delatour nodded sadly. The merriment faded from his brown eyes, as he lumbered to his feet and put an arm around Amy. "You like my *petite fille, hein, monsieur?*"

Martin nodded too, annoyed that he felt himself reddening, for he knew that the unsophisticated old man was seeing him as a possible suitor.

"I like her very much, as a *student*, I enjoy teaching her, she has a most original mind. She'll do you great credit when she grows up."

At those clearly dismissive words Pierre looked abashed, and Amy turned on Martin a long, surprisingly mature gaze in which there was reproach and defensive pride. "He likes me only as a guinea pig, Grandpère," she said. Then, as her grandfather looked worried, she translated, *"un petit cochon d'Inde* for scientific experiments," and she turned away

Martin withdrew in uncomfortable embarrassment. He walked up the avenue to the nearest bar and ordered a scotch and soda. After the second drink he decided to stop thinking about Amy, her disagreeable mother, or her arid home situation.

He returned to his Friday classes, again determined to ignore Amy, and was, therefore, taken aback to see her sitting at lunch in the Student Center with Mac Wilton, one of the most popular jocks in the school. Mac, a handsome, stalwart boy of eighteen, had his arm along the back of Amy's chair and was talking animatedly. Nor did Amy look up as Martin walked past to the Faculty Dining Room.

Martin refused to recognize so humiliating a pang as jealousy. But he thought about Amy and her strange remarks under hypnosis, as well as her assertions concerning the Bush-Holley House in Cos Cob.

That afternoon, before he went home he drove again to the Greenwich Library, and after consultation procured bound volumes of the Connecticut Colonial Records. While delving in the years 1755–56 he received a considerable shock.

In October 1755 the Connecticut legislature had "Resolved to accept neutral French inhabitants of the

Province of Nova Scotia" and a later entry in January 1756 said, "Distribution of the Acadians—Stamford 9, Greenwich 6."

"My God!" Martin cried out, staring at the musty faded page. "I'll be damned! So some of them *did* come to Greenwich!"

An elderly lady who was researching her ancestors in the next booth craned around in astonishment. "Sh-h," she said crossly.

"Sorry, ma'am," cried Martin, "but I've found the most extraordinary fact. I'll bet you never knew that six of the exiled Acadians were dumped on Greenwich in 1756. They were interned here. It *says* so."

The lady primmed her lips. "I don't know what you're talking about and can't imagine why, you're so excited. You're disturbing me." She averted her head, seized her ball-point pen and ostentatiously began to make notes.

Martin murmured another apology and was quiet while he stared at the sparse little items in the Colonial Records.

He was excited. Surely even Claire would be convinced by this evidence that Amy in her semi-dreaming or hypnotic states had known that there had been any Acadians here. Then he heard Claire's probable rebuttal. "*You* found the Colonial Records, why couldn't *she?* Hysterical subjects are very shrewd."

Nevertheless Martin did not think that Amy had discovered these items. Claire did not know the girl, she had not heard the tapes.

And now he wanted to see Amy again on Thursday night. He told her so after class on Monday morning, and to his dismay, found her hesitant. "Well . . . you know I'd like to come, but . . ." She stopped, biting her lips, a tint of rose flushed her cheeks.

"Oh, I know," said Martin. "You're worried about your mother, but she's accepted the lie—the seminar

—which isn't quite a lie, and I *am* trying to help you with your work."

"It's not that . . ." said Amy slowly. "Mother's beginning to find she can't run all my life like when I was a child, and in her own funny way I think she approved of you, certainly Grandpère did . . ."

"Well, then . . . ?" said Martin "I want to show you some really extraordinary information I've found about your Bush-Holley experience. We're on the track of something fantastic."

Amy swallowed and looked past him vaguely into the crowded Student Center. "You see," she said, "Mac Wilton's asked me to the hockey game in Darien, Thursday . . . nobody ever did before."

"Oh," said Martin, annoyed at the intensity of his disappointment. "Of course, you must go . . . how did you suddenly get so thick with Mac anyway?"

"Not so thick . . ." said Amy, who couldn't imagine why Mac had suddenly taken an interest in her, as she did not realize how much her manner and looks had improved lately. Nor that her experiences with Martin had produced softness and an attractive glow.

"Anyway," she said, "Mac's steady girl friend— that's Doris Drake—has got the flu and is home sick. I guess Mac just asked me on impulse, but I'd like to go. Do you mind?"

"Certainly not," Martin snapped. "Only I think we're approaching a real break-through on your problems —what about Friday . . . no, I've got a class myself in New Haven, and on the weekend I'm visiting Louisiana friends in Westport. We'll have to wait until next week."

"OK, I guess," said Amy. She gave him a faint smile and hurried off to her pottery-making class.

Martin knew it was unreasonable to feel dampened, but where had all her eagerness to be with him disappeared to? Her touching dependence, her open . . . well, almost adoration, which he was constantly keeping within bounds. Casual attention from that young hulk of a Mac Wilton should not have changed her like this, and was particularly annoying since the puzzle of her glimpses into the past was yielding some startling clues. Martin strode off to teach his Shakespeare class and did not handle his scuffling, whispering students with his usual patient courtesy.

Chapter Four

Mac Wilton duly confirmed the date with Amy to take her to the hockey game on Thursday night.

Getting permission from her mother for this date had been unexpectedly easy. Sarah was feeling better. She had not told anybody, for she hated admission of weakness, but she had dragged herself to the hospital clinic one afternoon, seen a brisk young doctor, whose questions she barely answered, but he prescribed medication which helped. Moreover, she had occasional inklings of how restricted a life her daughter lived. Mr. Stone's visit had made some impression.

And then she knew something of the Wilton family, who had a charge account at the department store where she worked. The Wiltons lived in a large colonial house up Lake Avenue, on the very site of an old Mead homestead—one visited by Sarah forty years ago. Mr. Wilton was a commuter and did business in New York. Mrs. Wilton was a pleasant and frequent customer to whom Sarah had sold several handbags and belts.

So Sarah's acquiescence, though characteristically grudging, came as a surprise to Amy, who was prepared to do battle if need be.

"Mind you come home the *minute* the game's over. I'll be waiting up, of course, and don't you let that boy take liberties neither, and don't ask him upstairs, don't want more disgraceful scenes with Mr. Delayter bellowing out French songs—bawdy, too, I shouldn't wonder—I can't think what that Mr. Stone thought of us, *he* had real nice manners." Sarah suddenly frowned. "I thought you went to Mr. Stone's seminar on Thursdays—"

Amy turned away. "Not *this* Thursday—" she said faintly. There was painful confusion when she thought of Martin.

"Well, don't skimp your classwork because you want to go gadding," said Sarah, "and if it was a movie you were off to, I'd certainly *not* give in so easy, and you be back by *ten,* and—"

Amy did not listen. She agreed to everything and finally went to her room, where she stared at the library copy of *Evangeline,* then at the few pages about Longfellow which she had scribbled out. She bundled Longfellow's poem and her own literary efforts into a heap and threw them in the bottom drawer of her dresser. She slammed the drawer shut with a bang.

On Thursday at six-thirty Amy was waiting at the window when she saw Mac's blue Porsche draw up on the street below. She wore her "best" dress, which was supposed to be reserved for Mead funerals or weddings. She, naturally, wanted to dress up for her first real date, and had no idea how inappropriate this was. Having been selected by Sarah, the dress was made of mouse-gray velveteen; unmistakably over-long and baggy, to allow room for growth. Amy freshened it up with bits of crocheted lace at neck and cuffs—heirloom lace, always kept wrapped in blue paper in a corner of Sarah's old pine chest, and its use would have been forbidden—but Amy did not ask.

Amy's last quick glance in the bathroom mirror rather pleased her. "Not so bad," she thought, removing her glasses and painting a timid thread of eyeliner around her lashes.

Her spirits soared further when she saw a spark of approval in her date's face.

"You look great, Amy," Mac said with some surprise, and he found her increasingly attractive on the ride to Darien, since she never interrupted once while he embarked on a long explanation of various football tactics in which he seemed to have made spectacular pays, or would have, except for idiocies perpetrated by the opposing team. Nor did he discover that Amy knew virtually nothing about football and still less of the hockey game they were going to. He had almost regretted his impulsive invitation, especially when his sister, an elegant young woman who went to Sarah Lawrence, twitted him about dating a "townie." The Wiltons were not snobs; still, Mac had never taken out a girl of Amy's background, and anyway, they all supposed him to be the exclusive property of Doris Drake, whose beauty was undeniable and whose parents belonged to the best clubs.

Amy enjoyed herself and managed to conceal the fact that without her glasses the wild antics on the skating rink where only hazy blur. She cheered when Mac did and enjoyed for the first time in her life the heady pleasure of "belonging."

When the game was over, four of the other seniors came up to Mac and he suggested that they all stop in Stamford for a drink.

"I can't . . ." Amy said nervously, "I'm under age and I promised Mother I'd go right home."

"That's ridiculous," said Mac, laughing, "you can have a *Coke*, me too, I'm still in training, and anyway, it's awfully early. There's a little shack off the Post Road where the guy plays a cool guitar when he's in the mood."

"I mustn't," repeated Amy in a weak voice of yearning. They were all staring at her as she stood by the entrance to the rink, the two boys with their

74

dates, none of whom she knew except by sight.

"Come on, Amy," Mac said impatiently. He tossed his head of curly brown hair, "Don't be a drip, I'll get you home at what any normal person would consider a decent hour. We aren't living in the dark ages. What could your mother *do* to you anyway?"

What indeed! Amy knew how ridiculous her hesitation seemed to the others, how incapable they were of knowing that she was assailed by panic, which did not really arise from conscience at breaking a promise, nor even from the impatience she saw in Mac's handsome face. Her fear was at once more subtle and yet sharper than that. It had the quality of warning and it brought the kind of inner quiver, or other-worldliness which came often with the feelings she had always called "dreaming true." And at the same time she felt anger. Why *shouldn't* she do as the others did, why not please Mac, the first man who had singled her out for attention, except Jeb, Jeb —and Martin Stone.

Amy straightened her shoulders under her old shabby blue coat and lifted her chin. "OK," she said.

Mac laughed at once, "Plays hard to get, this chick." He winked at the others. "Come on, then, let's go!"

They piled into two cars, Mac's Porsche and somebody called Red's Mercedes. They barreled down the Thruway and left it at a Stamford exit. They drew up at the small grimy bar and grill. The two rooms were dark, smoky, the tables lit only by romantic unshaded candles stuck in bottles. The place was jammed with young people, some dancing in tight embraces, some crooning along with the guitar player. Mac gave an oily little man a lavish tip and somehow a table was found for them in a corner. Mac ordered drinks, a Coke for himself and Amy, but the others had vodkas or whiskey. Amy stared at the flickering candle on their table as it wavered and sizzled a little. I won't be a fool, she thought, and drew as far from the candle as she could.

Mac politely asked Amy to dance, but she shook her head. She had no skill or practice at dancing. So he danced with a tall pretty brunette called Peggy who wore very tight blue jeans and a clinging rose sweater. Amy watched them exchange a long kiss on the dance floor. After that Mac seemed to lose interest in Amy, who huddled into herself and tried not to look at the candle. Her own glow had dimmed. She no longer felt that she "belonged," and when Red, after two strong drinks, suddenly lunged at her and fumbled with her dress, she reacted with an instinct she had never guessed she had. She slapped him on his startled freckled face.

"You little—" cried Red, staring at her and rubbing his cheek. "Hell, Mac, whatever made you drag this one along?"

"God knows," said Mac, who had returned to the table. He chuckled at Red's discomfiture. "Museum piece, I guess. Collector's item. Here, baby, have a drag, it might soften all this Yankee prudishness." He offered her a small brownish cigarette.

"Thanks, no," said Amy, at last realizing what kind of cigarette they were surreptitiously passing around among each other. "And I'm *not* Yankee, at least not the real me, I'm French!"

This produced a small bewildered pause.

Then Peggy Manson spoke, enunciating with drawling amusement. "I think you're weird, dear, real crazy." Whereupon they all giggled.

"Let her alone," said Mac, "she's just doing her own thing." He turned and cried. "Oh, listen to Gyppo, now he's playing a hell of a lot better!" The guitarist had gone into a slow poignant rendition of "Bridge Over Troubled Waters."

"I wish he'd play one of his own *new* ones," said Peggy critically. They all listened and hummed, while Amy retired even further from the table. Where *was* any bridge over troubled water for her? Her panic was growing. It almost stopped her breath. "Weird— real crazy." Peggy hadn't spoken with any heat, it was just a careless observation, yet if it were true . . . Martin swore he did not think so, but she hadn't wanted to see Martin tonight. She had been afraid of further probing into her inner "other" life.

"I've *got* to get home," she started to say—and then it happened. A swarm of kids rushed in through the door, which they did not bother to shut. There was a swirling draft. Some of the candles blew out, but the one on Amy's table licked sideways and caught the frayed edge of a thin sleazy curtain by the shuttered window. At once a ripple of fire ran up the curtain.

Amy stared at it and screamed. She felt herself surrounded by fire, she was suffocated by the smoke. She slid off her chair in a dead faint.

It was all over in a minute. Mac acted with the instant reflexes which made him an outstanding athlete. He whipped off the checkered tablecloth and its load of half finished drinks; he shrouded the curtain with the conglomerate mass, he tore down the curtain, which stopped flaming at once, leaving only a slight stench.

The proprietor hurried up with a pitcher of water, but it was not needed.

Few in the other parts of the rooms had even noticed. The guitarist went on plaintively wailing about the "Bridge Over Troubled Waters" and nobody at Mac's table even seemed startled, in fact, they laughed while Red said thickly, "Good thinking, Mac, but I guess we better get outa this mess, it'll take ages to clean up."

Mac said, "Yeah, this dive's getting boring anyway. We might try Lou's." It was then that Peggy noticed Amy, flat on the floor, half under the table.

"What's with *her?*" she said, pointing.

"Kid's passed out," said Mac, frowning, "though I don't see how. She didn't drink the Coke even." He knelt down by Amy and turned her over. He grabbed the pitcher of water and flung some of it on Amy's white, unconscious face. "Here, Red, she must need air. Help me get her out of here."

The proprietor was annoyed and worried about the fire laws, but nobody else paid much attention as the young men carried Amy outside. Mac, who had, of course, taken first aid, knew from her pulse and short sighing breaths that she was certainly alive, and when they reached the sidewalk she became conscious.

"I'm OK," she said, standing up shakily. "You see, it was the fire . . . I did see flames, didn't I?"

"Crazy, as I said before," remarked Peggy conversationally. "Take her home, Mac, and then we'll meet at Lou's, OK?"

"OK," said Mac, "see you later." Such a fuss about nothing, he thought. Yet Amy's frightened, confused voice disturbed him.

They bundled Amy into the Porsche, the others thankfully waved them onwards.

Long before they reached Amy's home on Greenwich Avenue she had entirely recovered. She even chatted a little about the hockey game and said how much she had enjoyed the guitarist. It dawned on Mac, who was very silent, that she had no memory of the trivial accident with the burning curtain, nor of her own fainting.

Mac was also preoccupied in deciding what story to tell the girl's mother, for it was now past midnight. There were many standard excuses, but in view of the energy crisis, running out of gas made the most sense.

No excuse was needed. They pulled up before the deli and saw a police car waiting in the next parking slot. Its lights were flashing and policemen were carefully easing a stretcher across the sidewalk.

"*Now* what?" Mac muttered.

Amy jumped from the car and ran to the stretcher. She gasped when she saw the grizzled beard and shut eyes. "Grandpère," she whispered, instinctively bending to hold him tight.

"Leave him be, miss," said one of the policemen. "Don't touch him! He'll be OK. He a relative?"

"My grandfather," said Amy in a strangled voice, "where's Mother?"

"Old lady's gone on ahead in a car. Maybe it's your mom. She'll be waiting at the Emergency Room. Stand back, miss."

Amy stood rooted to the sidewalk, watching as the cops deftly slid the stretcher into the ambulance. "No," she whispered, "No, no, *no!*"

Mac had never before heard anguish in any human voice, only pleasant things had been his lot during his eighteen years, and he was dismayed at all the annoyances of what should have been an ordinary little hockey date. Yet he certainly could not leave Amy like this on the sidewalk, moaning beneath her breath, trembling, and making queer little motions with her hands. He was only momentarily tempted to leave her, thinking of the gang waiting at Lou's. And what was a grandfather with a probable heart attack, after all—his own grandfather had survived several.

"Here, Amy," he said gruffly, "jump in, I'll drive you to the hospital. I guess you want to go and see the poor old guy. Or is there someone upstairs to take you?" He gestured hopefully up to the Delatour flat.

She shook her head and collapsed on the seat of the car. "I've *got* to see him. Oh *Mon Dieu, Mon Dieu, Sainte Vièrge, aidez nous!*" she suddenly wailed.

Mac hastily put the car in gear. "Weird" is right, he thought, "spaced out." The girl's voice had changed, grown deeper, as she gabbled unfamiliar words, which Mac assumed might be a prayer though he could not understand them, and she kept repeating them all the time he drove the short way to the Emergency Room of the Greenwich Hospital.

"Sainte Vièrge—Sainte Vièrge!"

The patrol car had just arrived, there was a bustle, flashes of white coats, the last wail of the siren still lingered on the chill November air.

Mac did not know exactly what to do and was immensely relieved to see a slightly familiar figure coming toward them through the sliding door. A tall thin man with a shock of light hair—one of the high school teachers.

"Mr. Stone!" cried Mac. "Mr. Stone!" He drew up near and shouted, "I've got Amy Delayter, she's kind of off her nut, worried, I guess, about her . . ."

"Yes, I know," said Martin. "I brought her mother here." He quickly examined Amy who was still wringing her hands and gabbling prayers in the Canadian-French accent of two hundred years ago.

"I'll take care of her, Mac," said Martin. "You go on—you've done your bit."

Mac smiled uncertainly and went.

The events of that night were never clear to Amy, though she stopped gasping out French after the charge nurse gave her a small tranquilizer. She sat with Martin and her mother in the waiting room while they performed emergency measures on old Pierre Delatour, then took him up to the Critical Care Unit. One of the aides brought in coffee, but Amy could not drink it. She did not wonder how

Martin happened to be there. Soon, when her mother stalked into the waiting room after consultation with the attending doctor, Amy looked at Sarah blankly, though she heard the sharp voice say to Martin, "I guess they think he'll do, but we better wait a bit. That Wilton boy bring Amy home *at last?* I'd certainly give her a piece of my mind, but I can see she's had a shock. She *is* fond of Mr. Delayter."

Amy heard this but she didn't understand it. She slumped back in her chair, shut her eyes, and at once she was on a ship clinging to the taffrail, for the ship was pitching and tossing. She heard the wind whistle through the rigging, heard sailors shout commands in rough foreign voices—English voices. The ship was heading southwest into the sunset. It was bearing her into exile—alone. *All* alone now, since someone very dear to her had died, on the ship. Someone was weeping. There was sorrow aboard the ship, grief as thick as the stench of tar, vomit, urine, and the kegs of fish pickled in brine. Only Paul could have stopped the weeping, but he was gone, too.

Martin and Sarah Delatour did not speak for some time while they waited. Yet Sarah was glad of Martin's company and more grateful than she would ever be able to express for his prompt response to her agitated phone call at eleven. She had already been angry at Amy's lateness, and the old man also showed concern. He stayed in the kitchen with her, drinking coffee. Then, out of the blue he gave a sudden choking cry, clutched his chest, and fell gasping to the floor. His face became a sweating gray-white.

Sarah, for the first time in her life, could not think straight. She ran downstairs to the deli owners, but there was no answer to her frantic knocks. She wondered whom to call and thought of her two remaining Mead cousins, but they lived in Cos Cob.

Doctor? She didn't know any by name. She stared again at the old man twitching on the floor, while his stertorous breathing seemed to blast through the kitchen. Then suddenly she thought of Mr. Stone. He had said he lived on Steamboat Road. Her fingers shook as she jerked through the telephone book; she eventually dialed the number.

It took Martin only a minute to understand her; then he acted promptly. He notified the police, called her back and said, "There'll be an ambulance. Don't touch him, ma'am, I'll be right with you." All the time Martin was conscious of tremendous relief that nothing seemed to have happened to Amy.

So here they were in the hospital emergency waiting room, an unlikely pair, but his apprehension had returned, for something *did* seem to have happened to Amy.

She looked to be almost in a coma though she was crying, and she had begun to mutter again in broken French sentences, while her arms moved constantly.

He summoned the charge nurse, who said, "Good Lord, we only gave her a tiny sedative, she shouldn't be like *this*. I'll get the doctor."

The doctor was baffled. There was no smell of alcohol on the girl's breath—his first thought, no evidence of drug poisoning either, yet they could not quite rouse her. They put her temporarily to bed in one of the emergency rooms where she lapsed again into silence, though she continued to make jerky, frightened motions with her hands.

"This beats me," said the doctor, "is she given to seizures?" he asked Sarah, who looked blank, so he said, "Does she have fits?"

"Of course not!" cried Sarah indignantly. "Meads don't have fits—nor Delayters neither, that I know of." But her gaunt face had melted into anxious softness, an expression Amy had never seen on her mother.

"Well, we'll have to admit her, keep her here overnight for observation, at least, and I've called an outside doctor since you have none of your own. Don't worry—nor about your father-in-law. He's responding well."

Martin and Sarah Mead Delatour continued to sit in the waiting room. Another emergency came in—sirens, bustle, the whole efficient machinery of aid —or survival—went into action near them. Several worried members of families gathered. One distracted husband talked incessantly. His wife had been out with some other guy, there had been drinking, the wife was badly injured.

Sarah said nothing. She barely heard. Martin smoked his pipe and wondered what he was doing here amid sorrow, grief, fear, all of which had nothing reasonable to do with him personally. He wished, like Mac earlier, that he were out of the whole mess. Yet he could not go. And, of course, when they were given clearance, he must drive Mrs. Delatour home.

They waited.

At 3:00 A.M. a pretty blonde nurse stuck her head through the door. "You the Delayters?" she asked, having identified a middle-aged woman and a tall, rather handsome young man.

Martin put down his pipe and said, "Yes."

"Better go back and get some sleep, we thought you'd gone maybe—Mr. Delayter's doing OK in the Unit, and the girl's awake again, perfectly normal except a little confused. She keeps talking about 'Paul.' That her boy friend or something?"

Sarah stiffened. "She doesn't know any Pauls."

The young nurse smiled. Mothers often did not know such things. "Anyway," she said, "they're OK tonight, we'll take care of them, you can check in the morning—and we have your number. Oh, by the way," added the little blonde, looking at Sarah, "besides calling for Paul, your daughter keeps babbling about a fire. She had some shock with a fire recently?"

Sarah shook her head slowly. "She's always had a quirk about fires—but she's absolutely *normal*, why *you* know that, Mr. Stone! You said she was one of your best students."

Martin took a long breath. He had not imagined that the grim Mrs. Delatour was capable of showing so much concern. She does love her daughter, he thought, and has never been able to show it.

"An excellent student," he answered Sarah quietly. "Quite gifted, and I suppose her behavior now—"

"Oh well," interrupted the nurse, for there were other emergencies waiting, "a touch of hysteria, we see it all the time. They might get a psychiatrist in the morning."

"Never . . ." said Sarah, clasping her handbag and standing up. "There's no money for such nonsense."

The nurse shrugged and smiled professionally. "Bye now," she said, and hurried away.

Martin drove Sarah home in complete silence. At her door she said a strangled "thank you" and disappeared up her staircase.

Martin went to his flat and could not sleep for the remainder of the night. He thought about Amy, not only the puzzle of her condition, to which he had certain clues, but about Amy herself. Her white little face as she sat in the waiting room before they took her back for examination. A face that for all its mute suffering had a strange beauty. It had evoked tenderness and pity. There was guilt, too . . . maybe if I hadn't started all that hypnosis, if I'd listened to Claire . . .

At seven-thirty the next morning he checked with

the hospital, found first that Mr. Delatour was doing very well, then the casual voice told him that Miss Amy Delatour seemed fine and might be discharged if the doctor approved, but the psychiatric clinic was recommended.

Then he telephoned Sarah, who had already checked herself and had reverted to her normal fretful tone. "Yes, I know—and Mr. Delayter's all right where he is, though who's going to pay for all these shenanigans I *don't* know, though I guess Medicare —as for Amy, I suppose I'll have to explain to the store and go get her. If she's that well, she can walk home, 'tisn't far, but I don't suppose she's up to school today...."

"Mrs. Delatour," said Martin slowly, "*I* can pick her up around noon, if you'll allow me to, and I can bring her to my home for a while and watch her— I've—there's a friend of mine who would be there."

Silence, while Sarah digested this. "Well, I'm sure that's very kind . . . take all that trouble. If she's not really sick she could stay alone until I get home— what a fuss about—"

"No," said Martin with slow emphasis, "Amy is not as well as you think. I believe I—we—can help her. I have considerable psychological training and I ask you to trust me."

He spoke with authority and Sarah, who knew that her job was in jeopardy, that her age and her frequent bouts of crippling pain had been reported to the head of her department, had a flash of relief. She wouldn't have to get time off again. And the Christmas rush, too. They'd hire young temporaries, but some of them might stay on—they wouldn't be apt to lay off an old employee before Christmas, but they *might*— it had been done. And if she was laid off, who would support Amy, or even Mr. Delayter. Sarah was perplexed as she never had been. This was a new world, which she did not comprehend. The certainties had evaporated. And now the specter of Welfare. That a *Mead* should go on Welfare—the proudest family in Greenwich, almost the oldest. She said, "Do as you think best, Mr. Stone."

There was a quaver in her voice, and Martin, who had so disliked the woman, heard it.

He thought of his own mother, Azilde, secure, languid, gracious, in her Bellerive, the historic showplace on the Bayou Teche, widowed now but still surrounded with luxury and attentive servants. Still lying in bed until ten or eleven, when the old butler would bring her a heavy brew of roasted New Orleans coffee with a buttered roll. Azilde was still wondering, though gently, why her adored son, her only child, would *want* to go up north and be a Yankee school teacher, or be a teacher at all. Why he had never taken an interest in the lovely Louisiana girls she used to ask to Bellerive. Ah, indeed, Azilde had always been living in what Claire had called "magnolias and moonlight." And this poor woman at the other end of the phone, Martin thought, such has certainly not been *her* lot.

"I'll take care of Amy, ma'am," said Martin. "I believe I can help, but I'll come up now and get an official release into my temporary care. Perhaps you'd better call me 'cousin.' "

"Land's sake," said Sarah, "but you *aren't!*"

"Never mind the 'cousin' bit, just give me authority."

"All right," said Sarah, as a twinge of sciatica gripped her right thigh. She hesitated a moment, "You don't think there's anything really wrong with Amy, do you? Until lately she's always been quite a *good* girl. But the Delayter blood . . ."

". . . Is as sane and staunch as your own, ma'am. In the *future* I think you must accept the fact that half, or maybe more, of her genes come from the French-Canadian side. And that you must also accept the fact that your son, who was more like *you,* is no longer here. Except by prayer, perhaps—you can do nothing for the dead. You *can* help the living."

Sarah gasped. "How dare you, Mr. Stone . . . and . . ."

Martin interrupted. "I *do* dare. I'll be up in five minutes for the release."

Sarah did as Martin wished. She telephoned the hospital, she wrote a note, then permitted Martin to drive her to the bus stop. He did not wait for whatever thanks Sarah might have tried to voice. He was almost late for school and would have to find a substitute for his Friday afternoon class—only one, fortunately—and it was not hard to arrange.

Mac Wilton was sitting with a group at a table during his luncheon block in the Student Center and came up as Martin was hurrying through. "How's Amy, Mr. Stone? Haven't seen her in school today. Gee, I felt bad about the kid last night, she said some pretty hairy things, and then in the Bar & Grill she kinda passed out, fainted. There wasn't any reason, I swear, except a curtain caught fire for a second. It seemed to bug her."

"Oh, indeed," said Martin slowly. "Well, Amy's doing all right now." Martin considered the big attractive boy with his broad shoulders and wide ingenuous eyes; innocent eyes, which showed little of the maturity Mac undoubtedly thought he had. "I hope you gave her a good time last night, I mean before the ending with the ambulance and all that."

"I guess so, at first," said Mac, "I dunno—Amy's different, but there's something about her . . . kinda sweet . . ."

"No doubt," said Martin curtly, nodded and hurried on.

He had no trouble extricating Amy from the hospital. She was already discharged, sitting again in the Emergency waiting room, looking oddly blank, yet composed, in her gray velveteen dress with its touches of lace at collar and cuffs. She had combed her hair into soft waves on her shoulders, she was pale, and her large eyes had a distant unfocused look.

"Hi, Amy," said Martin cheerfully. "We're leaving. I'm going to take you back to my apartment for a while. Your mother says it's OK."

Amy seemed to gather herself together from a long way off. She shrugged a little. *"Comme vous voulez,"* she said, then, repeated carefully in English, "As you wish." She turned and stared out of the window.

Martin went and checked with the morning nurse. "She doesn't seem quite with it. Do they think there's anything wrong?"

"Oh no, I'm sure not. She's been discharged," said the nurse rather impatiently. She was deep in papers, sorting admissions, diagnoses, referrals, case histories —and a new car crash reported coming in any second. "One of the volunteers took her up to see her grandfather for five minutes this morning, because she insisted. He's doing fine, I believe."

"Thanks," said Martin. He started as he heard a commotion outside, saw a stretcher come through the sliding door, and hesitating a moment, heard the initials, "D.O.A." murmuring through the hall. He knew what they meant: Dead on Arrival.

That's the end of somebody, Martin thought, as he went back toward the waiting room. But is it really the end? Forever? Or, as his mother thought—or accepted—for Martin knew that his mother had never troubled herself to question anything she had been taught at the convent—was there a delightful realm of pink clouds floating near the glorious throne of the Almighty—for some. Or a hell, full of demonic tortures, presided over by Satan, for the damned? Martin did not think so. There was no proof of such a hereafter. No proof of *any* hereafter . . . except . . . well, was there any proof of living in the here-to-fore? The past? *Why* is Amy so terrified of fire? Which century is she *really* in? And why?

He went and retrieved the girl. She greeted him politely, as though she scarcely knew him.

Maybe a psychiatrist on Monday, he thought, but in the meantime—the weekend.

When he got Amy back to his flat he fed her a hamburger and some milk, then suggested that she lie down for a while on his divan. He covered her with the Navajo blanket. She immediately went to sleep.

Martin telephoned Claire. He got her on the second try. "Look, honey," said Martin in the Louisiana drawl which they both had grown up with, "I expect you think I'm a heel, and stupid, too, but I've a situation here I want help with."

"Uh-huh," said Claire after a moment, "you've got in too deep with that little high school student you kept talking about."

"In a way, I suppose," he said, "but it's *not* sex, or I wouldn't call you. You deal with troubled kids, it's your job, and you must know a hell of a lot more than I do about abnormal psychology. I'm just a fumbler, only had two courses . . ."

"So what is it you want?" interrupted Claire crisply.

Martin explained with some difficulty and false starts.

"I get it," said Claire. "I'm invited for the weekend as a kind of chaperone—and again, you want to try an experiment."

"You always *did* have an extraordinary grasp of the essentials," said Martin with an edge in his voice.

There was a pause. Then Claire said in a softer tone, "You really want me, Martin?"

He said, "Yes."

"Well, I had a weekend lined up with some rather amusing people on Long Island, including a certain gent—the Charles I mentioned—but I suppose I *could* cancel."

"Please . . ." he said.

When Claire arrived on an afternoon train, Amy was still asleep on the divan. In fact, she had not stirred. But when they looked at her shadowy upturned face it seemed very flushed in the dim light. Amy's eyes were closed. She made a pleading sign of the cross with her right hand and murmured something.

"What's that?" asked Claire, in a whisper.

"Jésu et Sainte Vièrge, I think," murmured Martin. "She's still praying in French and *I* believe there's a reason."

"The child's sick, she's in shock," said Claire with startled pity. "She needs a doctor."

"The hospital discharged her," said Martin, "and you can't get the medics on weekends without gross emergency, and I don't know of any doctor who could handle this, anyway."

"You think *you* can?"

"Maybe, with your help. And I might say that I *don't* think she is possessed, and am quite sure she has not seen *The Exorcist* or even read any of that stuff. Nor do I believe in the devil, any more than you do. I think that Amy, due to many factors, including the fear about her beloved grandfather's sudden attack and her own efforts to lead a normal 1970's life, has slipped a time cog. She's *back* in time."

"Reincarnation again?" asked Claire, her delicate face hardened. "You haven't really fallen for that nonsense!"

"I haven't fallen for anything. I simply don't *know*.

But you might listen to a few indubitable *facts*. I'll try to express them briefly."

Claire nodded her sleek little black head and smiled. "I'm quite willing to listen, Martin, but you needn't be so fierce. And since you've asked for my help, and I have zeroed a weekend, which, I will say again and no more—included a guy I find most attractive—I canceled because of certain stronger promptings . . . our old friendship, your cry for help." She leaned back in the contour chair and fished out a cigarette. Martin lit it for her automatically, then suddenly smiled.

"So—OK, honey. What's the rest of the speech? You were a dear to come out here and I love that yellow blouse on you. It gives a glow, and—"

"Never mind the sweet-talking," she interrupted. "I was raised on it. We're here to do a job—to help this child, right?"

He nodded slowly. "And I defer to your instructions."

Claire glanced at the motionless Amy. "While you are giving me the *facts* as you know them, I suggest we go into your bedroom and shut the door, if there is to be any sort of scientific experiment. This girl may or may not be completely asleep. In any case, it would be foolish to let any suggestions seep through. I've had several dealings with hysterics and *you* have been fooling with hypnosis and know its suggestibility. Let's at least get a clear field. Bring the tapes and recorder in, too."

Martin immediately saw that she was right and felt a trifle foolish that he had not thought of this himself. He had never admired Claire so much and was ashamed of the sudden excitement in thinking about her in his bedroom. One did not, *should* not mix emotions, but this one took him by surprise.

The two of them actually were very businesslike.

Martin moved the apparatus. They shut the bedroom door and sat side by side on the king-sized bed.

"Now," said Martin, "it all began with Longfellow and his blasted *Evangeline*. Back in September— like this—" Martin recapitulated his first contacts with Amy. He told of subsequent meetings. Claire interrupted once or twice with a pertinent question. Then she was silent, her blue eyes slightly narrowed, her head lowered in thought as she listened.

She made no comment after he told her of Amy's "hallucinations" on Greenwich Avenue and at the Bush-Holley House. And then when she heard the tapes, she said only one thing, "Whoever 'Paul' was, the desperate love *does* seem to come through. Also, a sense of exile."

"Yes," said Martin, "and you can say 'adolescent fantasy' but listen to this. There *were* six Acadians allocated to Greenwich in 1756!"

Claire was definitely astonished. She had been more convinced than her practical mind condoned by Martin's account but she felt that it was all too incredible. Yet here might be proof. "Allocated where?" she said quietly. "And who were they?"

"I can't find out. I've been to the town archives. I've combed the libraries. Nobody knows, nobody ever heard of the allocation, but the Connecticut Colonial Records are there for anyone to read."

"H-mm," said Claire. "I begin to see why Amy fascinates you." She mused a while and lit another cigarette. "The New York Public Library might have something—or possibly Nova Scotian archives."

"I know, but there's not been time. Good Lord! Listen."

Through the door they heard a moaning, which suddenly rose to a muffled shriek. They rushed into the living room to find Amy cowering on the divan, her hands raised as though to shield her face and the hands had turned scarlet. They suddenly seemed to be covered with blisters, little watery welts.

"Le feu," Amy moaned, *"Ah, Seigneur, ayez pitié, aidez-moi!"*

Martin was too stunned with horror to move as fast as Claire did. Claire ran to the divan and took Amy in her arms.

"Hush!" she said. "Hush, dear, don't be afraid—it's not real—you're having a nightmare. *Wake up!"*

The girl trembled violently, she gasped twice, but she seemed to hear. She slumped back on the divan, her blistered hands fell limp. She lay quiet except for long shuddering breaths.

Martin and Claire stared at each other. "Gosh . . ." said Claire unsteadily. "I see what you mean by pyrophobia—you'd think her hands had been *burned.* It's like the hysterical stigmata one reads of; so-called saints who develop the five bleeding wounds of Christ every Friday—and oh, what the power of the mind *can* do to the body. Gosh, I'm shook myself. I—we—need a drink!"

He nodded, went to the kitchen and poured whiskey for both of them. They sat down at the table. After a moment Claire said, "No ordinary doctor, even a psychiatrist, would believe this tale. The usual hysterics, we slap them hard on the cheeks, we pretend to get angry. This seems different—*real* suffering."

"I'm glad you see it at last," he said. "Some curtain caught fire in the bar her date took her to last night; he says she fainted."

"And then the shock of her grandfather's near death right after," agreed Claire. "I give in, Martin, I think that *now* you should try hypnosis again, see if we can possibly get to the bottom of this . . . wait, have you any sedation here?" For Amy was still shuddering.

"Only some pretty good stuff they gave me in Viet

after I was wounded . . . I think there's a pill or two left."

"We'll try one on her," said Claire. "She's got to be calmed down or your efforts'll never work."

Martin finally located the pill vial, which he had stashed in the bottom of his old flight bag, then between them with great difficulty, they made Amy swallow half a pill.

"I can't," she kept moaning, "can't swallow—Oh, *Bon Dieu, aidez-moi . . .*"

"You can and *will* take this," said Martin. "Trust me, Amy, it'll help you and pretty soon you are going to talk to me awhile in *English*. Afterward you'll feel much better. You'll be *well*."

Somehow the pill went down. They watched as she gradually stopped shuddering, then Martin said quickly, "Please phone her mother's store—here's the number, tell her you're a doctor—which you *are*—of philosophy—that the hospital thinks it better Amy stay here for the weekend. *You* know how to handle difficult parents, I'm sure, and, mind you, ask for Mrs. Delayter. I had this in mind all along, as you guessed, but I did *not* guess it was going to be so hard."

Claire soothed Sarah Mead Delatour with efficiency. Sarah was worried, yet relieved. She got the impression of a much older woman speaking, and deeply buried were the doubts she was beginning to have as to how to handle Amy herself. Some of the ice had melted around her heart as she looked at her anguished child in the hospital emergency waiting room.

Claire returned from the phone. "That's all right," she said. "Now, you can get to work and needn't hurry. Wonder if your painkiller contains sodium pentothol, the 'truth drug,' it'd help make her talk. I've seen it used, it knocks out the inhibiting controls—but I'm scared, we're taking chances."

"I feel like praying," said Martin, with a twisted

smile. "But I don't know how to go about it, I don't suppose *you* do?"

"Not really," answered Claire, "yet, you know, I believe with William James that there is *something* we can call on in need and which will answer."

She put her hand on his for a moment and he instinctively leaned forward to kiss her. She brushed her lips against his cheek. "No, Martin," she said softly. "It's Amy who counts. My God, look—aren't there new red marks on her face?"

Martin peered down, saw the marks, and drew in his breath sharply. He turned off all the lights except the one in the ruby chandelier. He set the tape recorder and said, trying to keep his voice steady, "Amy, lie quiet where you are. Open your eyes and look at the light! You've done this before, remember?"

She opened her blank eyes and whispered, "Yes," through parched lips. He continued the routine. "Now you are quiet, you are relaxing, don't try to listen to me —just let your mind wander—and then when I count up to ten you will speak. You may hear another voice, a woman's voice—she is here to help you, too. Now, I'm counting . . ."

Amy spoke at the end of the count. "Mothers don't help . . ." she said in a small dragging whimper. "Mothers hate you or else they die and leave you alone."

Martin was startled, but Claire understood. "I'm *not* your mother, dear," she said. "I'm a stranger, only here to help you."

"Stranger?" said Amy, cringing. "They were *all* strangers—after they made us leave—leave Grand Pré. Horrible Yankee-English, they were cruel."

"Never mind," said Martin. He added with calculated vehemence, *"Did you ever find Paul?"*

The two spectators held their breaths. Amy took a long time to answer. She stared up at the light, then

95

suddenly her blotched scarlet face softened, she smiled a wistful, tender smile. "Paul found *me*. In Greenwich —after a long time. He'd been to Louisiana, and I'd *run* away twice, almost as far as New York. They brought me back—the constables—the Bushes traced me. I was their bond servant. Paul and I, were married in—in the big meeting house on the hill. The Meads let us get married. Dr. Amos Mead—*he* was kind. But his wife was a Bush, Mistress Ruth, from the old house in Cos Cob. The Bushes were mean. I slept with the black slaves. Candy wasn't mean—she died in the wash house, died all alone and screaming."

"Yes, we know," said Martin, who had told Claire everything of Amy's hallucinations. "Where did you and Paul live after you were married?"

Amy recoiled, she put her hands to her face. She was silent for a long time, then whispered. "He left me again—taking our little son, Pierre. He had to—he wanted to go back to Acadie, then send for me, prepare a place in our *own* homeland. He was never happy here, farming for Dr. Mead. He wanted his *own* land."

"Did you ever see Paul again?" asked Martin, very low.

She shook her head, a tiny motion. She began to cry, tears welling from her wide-open staring eyes and rolling down the blotched cheeks.

"I think she's had enough," Claire whispered. "Get her out of it."

He held up a silencing finger to Claire and said quickly, "Amy, why are you crying?"

Again Amy took a long time to answer, and when she did it was only partially coherent. "Waited so long at first . . . such a short time together . . . then he left . . . the years, years in our cabin waiting. Dr. Mead . . . another war . . . English enemy again . . . but one day Paul . . . sent for me . . . the Indian . . . Mishadoga . . . slipped through the lines . . . I was so happy . . . only a few hours . . ." Her voice got so low that they both strained forward. "Then it happened."

"What happened, Amy?" asked Martin in the calm soothing tone. The girl suddenly convulsed, she gave the same muffled shriek they had heard before, *"Non, non!"* she cried, *"Seigneur Dieu, ayez pitié."* She put her hands to her face.

"OK, Amy," said Martin, still quietly, though inwardly dismayed. "You are going to wake up now after I count. You will feel calm. You will drink a glass of milk, then go to sleep, and afterward awaken refreshed. You will remember none of this."

Claire and Martin watched with considerable anxiety, but the girl gradually stopped trembling. The wild blank look left her eyes. She sat up and accepted a glass of milk from Claire.

"I'm sleepy," she said in a high childish voice. "So sleepy." And falling back on the divan, curled up in the fetal position; her breaths grew even. But her hands were still blistered, her face mottled a livid red.

"Whew . . ." said Claire after watching a moment. "This is pretty gruesome. Let's not talk until we've had some food. What have you got in the fridge?"

They went silently to the kitchen and found that it was past midnight. They ate hamburgers and cheese. Claire made instant coffee. They spoke not at all, but Claire went in once to check on Amy, who seemed to be sleeping deeply.

Martin had been gradually seeing Claire in a new light, he realized an emanation from her, not only her undoubted attractions, nor her intelligence, but a quality of "goodness" tempered by "soundness"—both old-fashioned words, which he found difficult to accept. But there was more and he began to feel the "more" strongly. He said at last in a voice which he tried to make casual—"Since Amy's doing all right in there, I guess we'll have to share my bed—"

Claire looked at him thoughtfully for quite a while. "I wouldn't exactly mind," she said, "but tonight there are other things more important. A girl's sanity is at stake. I'm now convinced of that. We'll move Amy to your bedroom with *me*. And you sleep on the divan."

There was a long silence, while the percolator sputtered again.

"OK," said Martin after the pause. "You're right, I guess." He sat down at the kitchen table. "Now shall we review together what we *do* know, while it's fresh in our minds. Two heads are definitely better than one."

Chapter Five

Martin and Claire talked in the kitchen for over an hour. They talked of Amy and the hints she had given, either from her dream life, visions, or hypnosis. They tried to piece them together and Martin, who had been up extremely late two nights running, finally said, "Look, Claire, I'm bushed. I don't really know what we're dealing with, but you can't get around those blistered hands and scorch marks on the face. We both saw them. In the meantime, we'll be fresher after some sleep. All I know is that nothing that either of us was taught seems quite to apply."

Claire gave him a wan smile. "There's got to be a natural explanation," she said. "Or a set of coincidences."

"Explain it anyway you can," he said. "But we'll have to try for more clues."

She nodded silently. They went together and carried Amy into the bedroom, put her on the left of the big bed. The girl did not stir, her face and hands were still scarlet, and when Claire tried to make her comfortable —though she did not undress her—she saw that the girl's thighs had also turned an angry red. Then, just as Claire pulled the covers over her, with Martin watching, Amy spoke in the sad dragging whisper, "Tryon's Raid. General Putnam was visiting the Bushes . . . before he went to the tavern . . . the Tories, those cowboys . . . they had masks . . . they were devils . . . they *wanted* to kill. Nobody to help."

Claire and Martin looked at each other. "That make any sense to you?" Claire whispered. "Cowboys, yet!" She felt Amy's flushed brow and then her pulse. "She does not seem exactly feverish—except all those awful red welts. We'll *have* to find a doctor tomorrow."

"I'm afraid so," said Martin. "But I know a little of Greenwich history. General Tryon's raid was toward the end of the Revolution up here—1779, I think. He was British of course, and a brave old Yankee called General Israel Putnam was here defending Greenwich, when he saw from a tavern window the Redcoats marching on the Post Road from Port Chester. Putnam barely escaped by galloping his horse helter-skelter straight down that hill near the high school to get help from Fort Stamford. The Redcoats fired, but were afraid to follow that crazy route. The hill was much steeper then. Old Put got reinforcements and became quite a hero. Greenwich is full of things named after Putnam."

"You're maundering, dear," said Claire. "And now we have *cowboys,* for Pete's sake! The Wild West wasn't even known in the times you think she's reliving. Amy's been seeing too much TV. It's all ridiculous . . . oh, hush your mouth, Martin!" for she saw he was beginning to speak. "Go to the living room and I'll take care of her until the morning."

The rest of the night passed without incident. They all slept, Martin and Claire deeply, but Amy, without benefit of her usual incantation from *My Lost Youth* suddenly began to "dream true."

It started as always with happiness, walking down the little street in Grand Pré, smelling the fresh loaves in her basket, hearing the clack-clack of her wooden sabots on the haphazardly cobbled road, hearing the melodious notes from St. Charles's Church ringing the

100

first angelus. She paused a second for the prayer and crossed herself. She saw ahead beyond the church the lush apple trees around Paul's home. They were loaded with fragrant blossoms, for it was June.

She was burning with excitement, a tinge of shyness, and great desire for the coming moment when she would see Paul, whom she would marry next week. The priest, Abbé Chevreux, a good man, would then solemnize the legal contract, which had already been signed before the notary. There was to be a big feast later, with dancing, and then all the village would cheer them to their own home. She and Paul would no longer have to make "pretend" shelters on the beach. They could kiss each other wildly, sensually, without any trace of guilt.

Paul had built them a solid well-thatched two-room *chaumière* between Grand Pré and the Gaspereau River. It was wholly theirs—and the land! Many fertile acres behind the dykes, an orchard, even a few willows once imported from France clustering by the new homestead. Part of this abundance came from her "dot"— her dowry, a generous one supplied by her father; part from the Delatour family, and many extras like the spinning wheel, six pewter spoons, a feather quilt— from friends. Everyone gave, when a young couple got married. Everyone rejoiced when the marriage was so suitable and the pair so handsome and so much in love.

Usually the vivid part of the dream stopped there by the welcoming Delatour hearthside, surrounded by the laughing faces of Paul's parents and the younger children—Henri, Jean, and Clotilde—and the babies —they all drank mugs of honied breakfast cider and ate the warm loaves of rich bread she had brought.

Always after that the dream jumbled into disbelief, fear, anguish, and no details, but on this night, lying next to Claire in Martin's bed, the dream went on.

Now it was the golden light of early evening, waves

sparkling on the Minas Basin; the June sun would last for a long time yet in this Northland. She and Paul were sauntering hand in hand along the dirt road beside the borrowed oxcart; it was loaded with furnishings for their home—a plough, stools, iron kettle, piles of blankets, a loom. By the day of the wedding all their goods would be in place and waiting. They were talking animatedly about their plans—the cow byre was not quite finished. Paul had saved enough to buy a cow.

"In time we'll need most of the milk ourselves—for the little ones," he said, laughing his merry laugh and kissing her so suddenly that he disarranged her small white-winged cap. "Until then the LeBlancs and their fourteen children can use the milk, in exchange for some of their grain or vegetables, though we'll have a good harvest even this first year, I think. *Le Bon Dieu* smiles on us—*eh, ma belle?* We'll be the happiest couple in Acadie!"

It was then that Mishadoga came, suddenly appearing from among the pines to the south where they bordered the road. The Indian glided so softly in his moccasins that they did not see him until he stood directly in front of the ox and stopped the beast.

"Hola!" cried Paul in surprise. "I thought you were off trapping! But I *knew* you'd be here for our marriage feast!"

Ange-Marie smiled too, and giggled. She knew what a deep friendship there was between Paul and Mishadoga. Years ago when they were little boys Paul had saved the Indian's life by helping to free him from an overturned canoe while they were out fishing together. No Indian ever forgot a kindness—or an insult. The Indian children—who lived in a camp of bark wigwams farther down the Gaspereau—often played with the Acadian children. Two of the girls from Grand Pré had even married into the tribe.

But Mishadoga was frowning now, his black eyes

did not warm in greeting, and though he understood French he answered Paul in Micmac.

She saw her betrothed's face change, saw disbelief replaced by anger. "The bastards!" he growled. *"Now* what do they want of us!"

"Oh, what *is* it?" she cried. It was then that the fear began. The dream dissolved into confusion and only bits came back to her. The English—and the *new* English, the Redcoats—they were converging on Grand Pré, their muskets on their shoulders, bayonets fixed. Fierce-shouted commands in the foreign tongue. They went into every house. Into the church. They confiscated all the weapons in Grand Pré. They imprisoned the good old Abbé. They demanded that the church be denuded. They took it over for their headquarters. Colonel Winslow from Massachusetts seized the priest's house for himself. The soldiers camped all over the churchyard. They used one corner for a latrine, on top of the graves.

During most of Ange-Marie's fifteen years she had known vaguely of the trouble between England and France—somewhere across the vast ocean. She had seen head-shakings, heard mutterings from her elders. She knew without interest that the Acadians had been commanded to swear an oath of allegiance to the British Crown. And that they had refused, *if* the oath meant fighting France, from whence their forebears all came, or the Indians, who were their friends. Nothing happened. They became "The Neutral French" and though there were English living some place in Acadie she had never seen any. Tales of warfare meant little, were not nearly as vivid as the stories grandparents told around the hearth in the long winter evenings. Stories of the *loup-garou*—the wolf-man, or of Létiche—the pathetic white ghost of an unbaptized baby, or the Indian accounts of Glooscap, the Micmac god whose head touched the sky, who had used Cap Blomidon for his wigwam, the Minas Basin for his beaver pond. Glooscap had left in disgust when the white man came, but he would come back some day. The children always shivered with delight. Yet nothing really touched Acadie or disturbed the peaceful ordered life they lived on their luxuriant lands, reclaimed from the sea by the dykes and constant effort. They had been let alone for years.

In this dream there were no more consecutive glimpses. She knew only that in a short time nothing was left. The church was stripped of its altar and its statues of the saints—the men of Grand Pré were imprisoned in the church. Over four hundred of them, including Paul. And, of course, no marriage. They were all prodded and flung into the ships haphazard—families separated, although her mother was with her for a few days.

And the final glimpse—that heartbreaking moment jammed on the deck of a Yankee ship, as it wafted out from the Gaspereau River into the great bay—when she saw with certainty the very spot where the house Paul had built for them was burning.

Claire, in a blue velvet bathrobe, went into the living room at eight. She found Martin, still fully dressed, but touseled and yawning, on the divan. They looked at each other with startled intimacy.

After a moment Claire said, "That poor child has been crying in her sleep. I awoke when she clung to me, desperately, sobbing in her sleep. She's still sleeping—she's still covered with those uncanny red blotches—I think they're worse. And God knows what the pill we gave her may be doing. You've got to find a doctor . . ."

"I'll try," said Martin, slowly pulling himself together. She gave him a small baffling smile. "I'll make some coffee. Then we'll deal with the immediate problem. Amy's what I was invited out here for—remember?"

"Sure—yes, honey," he swallowed and unfolded his long frame. He ran his fingers through his straw-colored hair. "Shower," he said. "Can't clear my wits without one."

She nodded and went to the kitchen. They had each had two cups when they heard sounds from the bedroom. They both ran in.

Amy was moaning a little, she was staring at her blistered hands. She looked up and accepted the pair without surprise. "What's happened to my hands?" she asked, "they sting and my face smarts. I hurt all over. Don't you smell smoke? I can't breathe very well." But her voice was normal, it was the voice that Martin was used to hearing in class.

"Well, yes—" said Claire cheerfully. "I guess you've caught a kind of bug—plenty of flu around. You *must* have some vaseline," she said to Martin, "that, and I'll make an ice pack. Should have thought of it sooner. We'll get a doctor to look at you," she added to Amy. "Just relax, dear."

"Doctor . . . ?" repeated the girl with dawning memory, her eyes grew round, "Oh, but Grandpère! He's in the hospital!"

"And perfectly OK," said Martin, "or we would have heard, though I'll check. Nothing to worry about."

Amy subsided at once. She did not remember her dream. She felt strange, lightheaded, and yet comforted. Her elders were *not* comforted. While Claire provided ministrations for what seemed to be burns, but could not be, Martin phoned the hospital. Mr. Delatour was indeed responding well, they would probably move him down to a ward tomorrow. Martin finally talked to the morning doctor in charge of the Emergency Room, who said, "Bring the girl back here," until he heard Martin's muddled account of the symptoms. The doctor grew increasingly grave—all those red marks on the skin, eruptions, the disorientation. "Is there much fever?"

Martin did not know, had no thermometer, and the doctor clucked disapproval. "She might have scarlet fever, might be a peculiar form of erysipelas—both highly contagious—and we can't receive her here until we're sure. Look, Mr.—Mr. Stone, I'll get in touch with the authorities. I'll locate an M.D. somehow, but don't expect him until afternoon. Keep her quiet and force fluids. In the meantime, I gather you've been thoroughly exposed yourself—you and your friend—and I'd rather not see you in the E.R. We don't want to start an epidemic! Just wait there—and don't go out! I gather from the girl's chart there were no signs of any thing like this when they discharged her." He made another expressive and irritated cluck. "These young doctors—miss everything," he muttered angrily, and went on to say something more, but Martin hung up.

He went back and reported to Claire.

"So we're still on our own," she said quietly. "And I have a feeling"—she paused—"Amy'll *maybe* come out of this herself. She does not have to be sent to your contagious hospital—is there one?"

"I don't know," answered Martin.

"Well, *I* know," said Claire, "this is not a sickness of the body. I have come to know this, to be certain, no matter how it shows on the body, and I think we should do what Amy now wants."

"What does she want?"

"She's been telling me, while I greased her and fed her ginger ale. I think she may have a little fever, but not much. It's a fever of the psyche—the soul. I'm quite sure she is not contagious, though we might be taking an awful chance."

"What does she *want?*" repeated Martin.

106

"She wants to go to some place near the library, to have us take her."

"But that's nuts—" cried Martin. "The doctor said . . ."

"I know, but we won't let her near anyone else. And it won't take long, except one thing—a little longer."

"What?" Martin was exasperated, fascinated, confused.

"I'll keep Amy in the car with me while you consult that History of Greenwich you mentioned. Look at the *Revolutionary* dates, not earlier, as you did before. Look for Dr. Amos Mead, and look for cowboys."

"You've got to be kidding—" cried Martin. "You said yourself it was all ridiculous! My darling girl, I'm sorry I brought you into this . . . and, besides, the contagion, the medic said so—I can't in decency go handling books . . ."

"We'll buy a bottle of Lysol on the way," said Claire. "You can steep your hands in it, but there *is* no contagion of that sort. I am sure of this with a part of me I never realized I had."

Martin puffed on his pipe for a minute. They both listened while Amy gave great sighing breaths from the bedroom, then heard her say, "Let me go back there—where it happened. Horseneck Brook near the toll road—waiting so long—then the cowboys came— they couldn't understand me. I couldn't remember English—they thought I was jeering. *Please* let me go there—I've *got* to go there—"

Martin listened. He knocked out his pipe. "When did she say 'Library'? God, Claire, this is nonsense, but there *is* a Horseneck Brook."

"Now *you're* the one who has to be convinced," said Claire faintly. "She said 'Library' while you were on the telephone, and at *that* moment she was mostly in the present."

"OK," he murmured, "we'll go."

They bundled Amy into the little VW. Claire sat with her on the back seat. Amy was quiet. She still wore the gray velveteen dress with its touches of crocheted lace. Her bloodshot eyes continually turned to Martin as he sat stern and baffled at the wheel.

"You've got her partially hypnotized," whispered Claire, with a nervous laugh, "and I hope you'll never monkey around with this stuff again—and yet," she added to herself, "it may save her. Otherwise—long psychiatry, institutions, commitments . . ."

They waited while Martin stalked into the library and was gone for twenty minutes. The November wind blew cold and Claire put her arm around the girl, who shivered and murmured, *"Pitié, Seigneur, Pitié, Douce Vièrge, je pars demain pour trouver Paul qui m'attend . . . enfin . . . enfin. Toute les anneés si longues . . ."*

Claire shivered, too, but it was not from the cold. There was such pathos in the voice, which had deepened again. She understood the words. The plea for pity from God, from the Virgin—the yearning for Paul, who had at last sent for her to come home, after all the long years.

Martin came back from the library. He saw Amy's scarlet face, half buried against Claire's fur-clad shoulder.

"Amy is right," he said briskly. "A gang of hoodlums—worse than that—of riff-raff criminals, who marauded and murdered as they wished—on both sides —mostly Tory. They *were* called "cowboys" during the Revolution. Dr. Amos Mead spent many days hiding from them. It's all in the book. And Dr. Mead's homestead was over there on Deerfield Drive, near as I can make out."

"Yes," said Claire, "I thought so." Her arm tightened around Amy. "Listen, dear, look at Martin—at Mr. Stone. Open your eyes and look!"

The girl slowly obeyed.

108

"Tell her to lead us to the site of wherever it was her tragedy happened," said Claire.

Martin turned slowly around in the car. "You want to walk to some place, Amy?"

She nodded. "In those fields," she said. "See the cabin way down there among all those great elms?"

Martin and Claire looked. There was no cabin, there were no great elms, there was only the big new rectangular medical building of whitish concrete, only the whizzing of cars hastening up to the Post Road to catch the traffic light before it changed.

"Would you like to show us?" asked Martin. Amy did not answer, but she made a fumbling movement toward the car door.

Martin opened the door and the girl slid out. She began to run from the library parking lot. They hurried to keep up with her and protect her in the traffic as they crossed Deerfield Drive. Amy plunged into a small overgrown path between a nursery and the new medical building. They scrambled with her down through a tangle of asters and goldenrod until they finally reached the trickle of Horseneck Brook, before it went underground. Amy looked about her in dismay. She looked to the south nearer the Post Road. "Where's Dr. Mead's homestead?" she asked plaintively. "It was up *there*." She she pointed. "He was kind, he let us build a cabin. Of course, Paul farmed for him and I worked a lot in the big house and helped with the children. Mistress Mead—that *was* Ruth Bush —she got cross—I couldn't seem to learn much English." Amy paused frowning. "But then he had to hide—Dr. Mead—days and days—from the cowboys. Dr. Mead was rich and he fought against the Tories at Ticonderoga. Maybe Paul would have fought, too, but he wasn't here, he'd gone back to make a place for me up home on the West Coast—St. Mary's Bay, not Grand Pré—the English had it. He took our Pierre, who

109

was eleven and big enough to help him. He thought I'd be safe with Dr. Mead."

Amy suddenly sat down on a boulder near the brook. "It was *here*—the log cabin where I waited. These stones—that was part of our cellar, where we kept the potatoes."

Martin and Claire stared at a tumble of mossy stones half buried in leaves.

"The cabin isn't here *now*," said Claire very clearly, "what happened to it, Amy?"

The girl put her blistered hands to her crimson-streaked face. She made an eerie muffled sound. Claire turned to Martin in alarm while she clutched his arm. They both knew the risk they were running of a total psychotic break as a retreat from this moment of Amy's facing her terror head on.

There was a long silence beside the sluggish brook. The wind blew colder. Amy crouched on the boulder, her face hidden by her hands, and moaned.

"Look at me, Ange-Marie!" cried Martin. "Tell us what happened here so long ago. *Tell us*—get it out!"

The girl raised her head. Her eyes met Martin's pitying gaze. She moistened her lips. Then they opened wide as for a scream—yet no sound came out.

"It's like a movie, dear," said Claire in the firm tone she used for disturbed children. "It's not real, you know, just something you can look at and then tell us the story about." Again there was silence, until Claire and Martin had almost given up hope.

Suddenly Amy spoke in a loud defiant voice.

"There were three of them—the cowboys—they wore black masks. They were drunk. They were looking for Dr. Mead. I tried to hide in the cellar. They found me. They dragged me upstairs—up the ladder. They had muskets. I couldn't speak to them. I thought they'd shoot me. Instead they . . ." she shut her eyes. "They had a rope. They trussed me like a chicken and

110

threw me on the floor. They set fire to the cabin, they had a torch. They scattered all the hearth fire over our wooden floor around me. They burned up the cabin and me in it. I got my hands free to shield my face, but my clothes had caught. It took a long time. As they left they laughed. I screamed and screamed, but nobody came."

Though they had both half expected something like this by now, her listeners shuddered. Claire's eyes filled, but she recovered first. "Good girl!" she said. "Now you've told us. And it happened *two hundred years* ago, Amy. It does *not, cannot* affect you now. It must be forgotten like any nightmare. You know how silly nightmares seem soon after you wake up?"

Amy gaped at her. The mists were clearing in her mind. She looked at the two concerned faces and her own grew puzzled. "What in the world are we doing here?" she asked. "Is it a picnic? It seems very cold for a picnic."

"And so it is," said Martin. "We'll go right back to my place. I'll buy some food to bring in, that'll be more fun."

Amy bowed her head and they each took one of her arms. They walked up the wooded path and across Deerfield Drive to the VW waiting in the library parking lot. They were all silent, until the girl spoke. "I guess they'll let me visit Grandpère a while this afternoon? And I wonder how Mother's doing without me. I always vacuum on Saturday mornings, because her legs hurt her. But I've got to baby-sit for the Robinsons later."

Claire and Martin exchanged a quick look over Amy's head. Certainly this speech was rational. They had taken a chance, and *surely* they had won.

Yet they were not entirely certain until they all got to the flat, which was chilly, the thermostat was turned

111

down, and they had forgotten to raise it during the hectic morning hours.

Amy looked at the fireplace. "Could you light it?" she asked Martin. "Have you enough wood? I'm sorry, but I do seem to be very cold and hearth fires are so pretty—at least," she looked puzzled again, "at least I've always read so."

Martin silently got the paper, kindling, and wood. When he came back Claire drew him to one side. "Look!" she whispered.

Amy's scarlet blotched face had faded to pink. Her hands, though still red, had ceased being lumpy with blisters.

"We *have* won," Martin whispered back. "We—and Amy herself, surely we've won! Thank God!"

He gathered Claire up against him and kissed her exultantly.

Chapter Six

Amy went to the last big football game of the season as Mac Wilton's date. At least, he got her a ticket on the fifty-yard line, and she sat with his parents who thought her quiet but sweet—and really an improvement over Doris Drake, who had recovered from the flu and did her cheerleader cavortings with blatantly sexy enthusiasm.

The Wiltons were mildly pleased at their son's recent interest in Amy Delatour. They knew little about the girl, except that she stemmed from the old Mead family in Greenwich, and had a French-Canadian grandfather who had been very ill, but was now at home. They did not expect to understand all the mysterious fluctuations of their eighteen-year-old son's female attachments, but they liked Amy.

And Amy was perfectly dressed for the occasion. Claire had seen to that. A smart red pantsuit with a beige turtle-neck sweater, and a warm fake fur coat that looked like sheared beaver. Though it took much persuasion and tact to overrule Sarah's first indignant refusals of *any* kind of gift.

Sarah, at first mystified and suspicious that so much pains should be taken with her daughter, was given a stringently expurgated account of what actually had happened. Claire, who interviewed her in the Delatour kitchen, kept it vague. "A strange illness—all over now—I'm sure." Claire used a lot of long words:

"Abreaction" "Early trauma" "Adolescent fantasies not unusual" "Imaginative identification with past Meads, due to a need for acceptance," etc.

From all this, Sarah seized on one motif. She still thought of Claire as an M.D., and found her pleasant —if incomprehensible.

"Well—" Sarah said finally, "I guess Amy *does* get something from my side—way back in the Revolution, I think Dr. Amos Mead was my ancestor. I've never bothered to trace back through all the Meads, but my cousins in Cos Cob have the family tree. I remember they talked about Dr. Amos, and that he owned acres and acres of land along Deerfield Drive north of the Post Road. Except, how would Amy know that?"

How, indeed? Claire thought. How were any of the singular links from the past—explicable? But she had seen with her own eyes, and there *were* facts to prove that Acadian exiles from Nova Scotia had been allocated to Greenwich in 1756. Would it help Sarah to try and explain this? Claire thought rapidly, and decided, no.

"Well, Amy's read a lot of books," she said temperately. "She has great intelligence, mixed as it often is at her age, with fantasy. With make-believe," she amended, as her listener looked uncertain.

"She has this funny craze about Longfellow—the poet—" said Sarah, "even has his picture in her room."

Claire nodded. "I believe it looks like her grandfather, and some of the poems—well, Mrs. Delayter, I'm sure you can understand in view of her ancestry, why she was suddenly overpowered by *Evangeline* —indeed, you know, half the world was reading it in the last century."

"Never read it myself," said Sarah, "or if I did, in grade school, don't remember, but I tell *you*, Doctor, I get sick and tired of all the French jabberings in my home, and hankerings after a place Amy's never seen. *Nova Scotia!* 'Tisn't natural."

"No, not natural." Claire smiled her warm understanding smile, for she began to understand the mother's distress, her feelings of exclusion, her inability to share the temperaments of her daughter and father-in-law, and her ever suppressed grief for the son who was dead.

"But, many things," Claire added, "happen to all of us which are hard to explain. Mrs. Delayter—I think Amy's almost well now. But she *wasn't*. From now on, will you try to give her some freedom, and," said Claire slowly, "to accept and love her?"

Sarah's sallow skin flushed. "Of course I love my child, how dare you say anything else?"

"OK," said Claire, "then make her feel it sometimes, by letting her do as she wants—and by not resenting her grandfather. You might try loving *him*, too. He needs it." She gestured toward the bedroom where the old man could be heard snoring gently. "He's a good man—he's really in exile too, far from the country of his birth and heart. Look," said Claire rising from the kitchen table, "I know you aren't well yourself, Amy told me. She feels for you more than either of you realize."

Sarah swallowed. She blinked back the shameful tears. Many years of resentment and self-pity were involved, but she was not going to show it to this strange young woman doctor.

"Thanks," she said curtly, "I guess you mean well by Amy. It would seem so. I was never sure that child would turn out all right, but mebbe something's changed, and I wish you'd *go* now."

"Yes, I will," said Claire. She took Sarah's hand, who at once withdrew hers in embarrassment.

"I'll do the best I can," said Sarah. "It isn't easy.

. . . I never should 'a married Pierre, he was so different from the other boys—I dunno—"

"Exactly," said Claire. "And long ago, too. Now, as I think Martin Stone once told you, *you* and Amy must deal with the *present*."

Sarah went at once to the sink, attacking the dishes with a clatter.

Claire looked at the defensive back in its blue and white print nylon. "Good-by, Mrs. Delayter," she said softly.

Sarah did not answer, she did not turn around. Claire let herself out the door, and went downstairs past the delicatessen.

It was on a Wednesday evening in mid-December when Amy suffered a shock which further changed her life, but she had no premonition, very little awareness of how much she had already changed. Fears and strange dreams had all stopped, it now seemed impossible that she had ever had them. The only tunnel she had ever been through was on the highway near New Haven, when she had made her defiant, hitchhiking trip a year ago to see Longfellow's Craigie House at Cambridge, Massachusetts. She no longer remembered the emotions which had prompted that two-day trip, but she remembered the tunnel, and how, after darkness, one suddenly came out into full sunlight at the end of it.

She had the same impression about her life, but she neither analyzed nor dwelt on the impression. She did know that she felt grateful warmth toward Martin Stone and Claire, and even some sympathy for her mother, whose nagging voice no longer infuriated her quite so much. But she did not really think at all. The sunlight had to do with Mac Wilton. She came alive only when she was with him, as she was this Wednesday noon.

116

At school their lunch blocks usually coincided, and it had gradually become the natural thing that they should sit together, among the group of seniors who always gathered around Mac.

Mac even softly strummed his guitar and improvised songs, just for her, while Doris Drake, after an indignant appraisal of the new situation, had finally shrugged, enslaved another jock, and formed her own group nearer the window.

"I wish I was as pretty as Doris is," Amy said involuntarily, having watched this maneuver.

"Oh nuts," said Mac, quirking his mouth. "Blondes don't really turn me on, besides, you're a good-looking chick yourself. And I like to talk to you. Doris doesn't talk, she operates."

Amy smiled, a charming, dimpled smile which transformed her by erasing all the anxious tensions, the impression of sulkiness she used to show.

Jeb Jones was wandering by toward the cafeteria with a pretty little junior whose olive skin and soft brown eyes showed her Italian extraction, and caught the edge of the smile. He paused uncertainly. "Hi!" he said, looking at Mac who had just executed some complicated chords on his guitar and was pleased.

"Hi yourself!" said Amy, realizing that she had seen almost nothing of Jeb these last weeks, but then she remembered very little of the past weeks. It was one of the peculiar things Claire and Martin had told her not to worry about.

"Want to join us?" asked Mac amiably. "Bring your lunch back here?"

"Sure," said Jeb after a startled moment. None of the "big men on campus" had ever specially noticed him before. They hadn't been mean, they just hadn't noticed him, and actually the few blacks in this school kept very much to themselves, except the basketball players, and Jeb was no athlete.

"This is Rosa DeLuca," said Jeb, thrusting forward the shy, giggling girl who clung timidly to Jeb's hand, and stared in awe at the famous Mac Wilton.

"Pleased to meet you, Rosa," said Mac. "Aren't we, Amy?"

Amy nodded, and blushed at this implied admission that she was Mac's steady date whose opinions counted. She thought with excitement of their date tonight. Mac was going to take her out to a restaurant, then they'd come back to his house. Just the two of them, which was rare. Her heart beat fast at the thought.

There wasn't much left of the lunch period when Jeb and Rosa came back, but Jeb had time to whisper into Amy's ear. "I think I got a scholarship and student loan to U CONN for next fall. . . . Mr. Stone's been helping. He's a good guy after all."

"Why, that's great, Jeb! Terrific!" Amy was startled to think of Jeb going on to the University of Connecticut, pleased for him, but it also touched off a sudden quiver of anxious envy. Her mother, though softer in some respects, was still adamant on no college for Amy. And, indeed, Amy was beginning to realize that her grades had been slipping during the long blurred past weeks. She seemed to have lost the knack of concentration, except on Mac. She had never turned in her independent studies paper about Longfellow, she had never finished the pottery bowl she had started in September, and strangest of all, she was floundering in French which had always been so easy. She garbled and misspelled written sentences, and when it came to speaking it now, she stammered, then was tongue-tied.

Amy had no idea that she had been the subject of several grave consultations among her teachers, nor of Martin's steady championship and pleas to wait before disturbing her, nor, of course, that he had incurred considerable criticism by his attitude.

The next afternoon, after school, Martin was summoned to the housemaster's office and again confronted by the frowning housemaster, who said that the guidance counselor had been unable to "reach" Amy at all; that the girl smiled vaguely, and simply did not listen.

"That girl's got herself very shaky Ds this term," said the housemaster, "even French would be an E, except for past performance, and stick up for her as you will, Stone, I see she's not doing well in English, either, *your* course." The older man's scowl deepened. "What's the matter with her? Sudden attention from Mac Wilton addled her brain? Or is she going psychotic again like that eighth-grade business?"

"No!" said Martin explosively. "She's had a lot of home stresses, give her time—and you must admit that her appearance has greatly improved."

"I do," said the housemaster dryly. "Stone, it seems to me that you take an undue interest in this girl. You're a good teacher and this is a lax moral era we live in, but the school would have to put a decisive stop to any fooling around like that. *Immediate, decisive stop,*" he repeated, tapping the table angrily with his pen.

Martin flushed, perfectly understanding the threat of dismissal in disgrace. He rapidly considered telling the whole story, and at once realized that he couldn't. Who would believe or condone the hypnotic sessions, the evocation of what seemed to be a past life over two hundred years ago—the pyrophobia, the sudden burns and welts for which there was no reasonable explanation, or the terrible and pathetic scene by Horseneck Brook. They'd send *me* to the loony bin, Martin thought, looking at the disapproving face across the table, or have me up for corrupting the morals of a minor. Those hours alone in my flat—Jesus! He drew a sharp breath.

"My fiancée and I *both* take an interest in Amy,"

119

Martin said crisply, over an interior shock. He certainly hadn't asked Claire to marry him, nor thought of anything but an all-out affair, though considerably miffed recently that despite their intimacy while they were helping Amy, and his impression that Claire was attracted to him, she had always evaded physical contact. He hadn't even seen her in ten days; the two times he tried to phone there was no answer. Oh, to hell with her, he had thought, not for the first time.

"Fiancée!" exclaimed the housemaster, startled and relieved, "Didn't know you had one, but we prefer teachers to lead regular lives, sets a good example —getting married soon?"

Martin flushed. "I—I guess so," he said, feeling like a fool, and then proceeded rapidly. "She's a Ph.D. in psychology, works with troubled kids. She thinks, and I think, Amy will pull out from this dreamy, no-achievement phase—and at least, the girl's happier than she was."

The housemaster snorted. "The 'happiness' may be marijuana or worse, far as *I* know. I've seen this slap-happy, drifting behavior too often; and she'd *better* pull out next term, or drop out. We have our standards. Far as I'm concerned, she needs psychiatric help, but you keep bucking that—afraid she'll talk too much?" he added, his eyes again suspicious.

"Of course not." Martin found himself flushing again. "Good God, I tell you I'm engaged. I just don't think Amy needs psychiatry. She'll shape up," he added faintly with a confidence he did not quite feel. The housemaster had punctured it. Amy had improved in so many ways, a tragic ghost was laid for her, she obviously bloomed under Mac's attentions, but Martin was compelled to face the fact that scholastically the girl was not "with it." She drifted through classes like a zombie.

Martin's thoughts were gloomy as he drove off in

his VW after school let out. What possessed him to say that about Claire? He had never considered marriage with anyone, except in some indefinite future, if he wanted kids—and to please his mother. And as for Claire, he had come to doubt the attraction to him she had seemed to show. Probably that Charles, whoever he was, was now making time with her.

In fact, Martin doubted everything as he crept with the traffic down Greenwich Avenue toward his apartment, guiltily aware that cowardice had made him claim a fiancée he did not have.

But, he thought despondently, it was self-preservation, since I couldn't tell the real reasons for my interest in Amy, and I *don't* want to be kicked out like that. Damn it, I like teaching at Greenwich High, and I've never had a blot on my academic record.

He unlocked his door and was greeted by the aroma of heavily roasted coffee with chicory, like the smell of the French quarter in New Orleans. There was also a whiff of something baking with cloves, peanut butter, molasses.

"What the hell . . ." he said, frowning, for he heard a clatter in his kitchen. He strode to the door and saw Claire, intently basting a small ham. She looked up quickly and made a rueful face.

"An impulse," she said, reddening at his stare, which seemed anything but pleased. "I hope you don't mind, but my afternoon classes were canceled, and I thought you might like a real Louisiana dinner. See, I've made us a gumbo, and there's our own kind of coffee—have a cup? I brought all the stuff from town," she added nervously, for he continued to frown.

"Of course I don't *mind*," said Martin slowly, still staring. She was touseled and flushed, her neat cap of glossy black hair had swung loose into little curls on her cheeks, and a dish towel was pinned around her slender waist over the expensive bottle-green suit. The

121

slight dishevelment made her look very charming—and different.

"How *did* you get in?" asked Martin, whose chest had begun to quiver with a mixture of anxiety and excitement. "I've got the only latch key."

"The super let me in, he's seen me around enough."

"Not for a while, he hasn't! I've tried to phone you, but no answer. I'd decided you were easing me out, now Amy's problem doesn't occupy you. Though maybe it should—the girl's failing all her subjects."

"Oh, Lord . . ." exclaimed Claire with a sigh.

She did not want to hear about Amy just now, but she answered him carefully. "I'm not surprised, really, though I hoped for the best. Amy's weathered too many shocks in too short a time. She's barely convalescent emotionally." Claire began to sprinkle brown sugar and cinnamon on the canned yams she had sliced ready for the broiler. "A total change would do Amy good, I think," she said. She glanced up at Martin under her thick black lashes, an enigmatic look.

Martin reddened without knowing why. He went and poured them both a scotch and soda. She refused gently and drank some of her ignored coffee. He gulped his scotch fast while his neck grew hot below the wavy, thick blond hair.

"I've a confession to make," he said roughly, "and for God's sake please quit that cooking for a moment, much as I appreciate it. Come into the living room."

Claire gave an uncertain little laugh. "OK," she said. She took off her dish-towel apron, smoothed her hair into place.

Martin poured himself another strong scotch and they settled on the living room divan, sitting decorously far apart. Outside the big window the harbor looked gray and frosty. A solitary sea gull mewed, then swooped out to the Sound.

"Confession all that hard?" asked Claire lightly,

glancing at Martin's second scotch. "I presume you haven't been robbing a till, or gone in for rape, or become a junkie, wait—perhaps you've found another girl student to hypnotize."

"None of those," he said, scowling down at the rug. "It's to do with *you*. I've made a donkey of myself."

"Oh?" Claire became very still and pale, noting with annoyance that her hands were trembling. She took a cigarette from her bag, and lit it. "Well, go on."

"It began with Amy," he said in a muffled voice. "They've had me on the carpet for defending her, they think I've been taking 'undue interest.' The housemaster practically threatened me with instant dismissal—they fired a male teacher last year for—" he stopped.

Claire compressed her lips. *Amy* again! She liked the girl, had been very glad to help her out, but it was not because of Amy that she had made herself unavailable for ten days, then when the longing to see Martin grew unbearable, she had canceled classes, bought food, and jumped on a train armed with one of the oldest feminine ploys. "The way to a man's heart is through his stomach," her mother used to say complacently.

"What's that to do with me, Martin?" she asked, keeping her head averted.

Martin still scowling at the rug spoke in a rush. "Well, you see I was chicken, and for Amy's sake, too, I couldn't explain—you know that—not to that suspicious old guy, so I said *you* and I were helping Amy, and I claimed you for a fiancée, said we'd be married soon. It was *unpardonable!*"

Claire looked quickly at his embarrassed face, then away. In the apartment there was a long silence, except that sleet began to hiss against the window.

At length Claire spoke in a small voice. "*I* don't find it unpardonable, Martin, except that you obviously didn't mean it."

His wits were slightly fuddled and it took him a moment to understand this. He transferred his scowl to her face which was tender, vulnerable, subtly beseeching—as he had never seen it.

"You mean you'd *like* to marry me?" he asked incredulously. "I thought you'd be angry—and what about the other guy, the one you told me about?"

"Oh yes, Charles—he's very fond of me, his intentions are serious, as we used to say in New Orleans, but I don't happen to *feel* for him." Unconsciously she put her hand over her heart, and to his astonishment, he saw her bright sapphire eyes cloud with tears. The poised, incisive Claire suddenly looked like an unhappy little girl, and in that moment Martin's defenses crumbled.

He drew her silently into his arms and began to kiss her. At first tenderly, then with mounting desire. She responded, nestling against him, though the tears spilled over and ran down her face. But she freed herself determinedly. "Oh, sure," she said half laughing, half sobbing, "I'd *like* to go to bed with you, but I don't want *just* that. I happen to love you, you idiot. For keeps. I have for a long time, and—" she added with a touch of the usual Claire practicality, "we have the same interests, and I think could make each other happy."

Martin hesitated, while her sincerity pierced through and calmed the rampant physical urge. "I think so, too," he said in a wondering awed tone. "It just never occurred to me—marriage." He kissed the top of her head, "But you know, I'm beginning to like the idea." He picked up his scotch then put it down untouched. He turned again to look at her, "Yes, I do like it, only, if you're going to turn into an ante-bellum flower of the old South, and hold off my bestial passions, let's get married *soon!*"

"Sure," she said, with a long sigh of the ecstatic relief which comes but seldom in a lifetime.

Martin having taken the plunge, felt himself suddenly and utterly content. A new sensation. They lay for a while in each other's arms, kissing and murmuring, deep in their timeless moment, until there came a sizzling spatter from the kitchen.

Claire jumped up. "Oh, darling—the ham! Maybe the oven's on fire—the grease!" She ran to the kitchen. He stayed quietly on the divan, thinking.

She came back soon. "It's OK. This *will* be a celebration dinner!"

"Uh-huh," he said, "and it smells great. But look, my love, you know what? Christmas vacation next week. Let's fly home, to my mother's, she'll put on a beautiful wedding at Bellerive. And *you've* no parents left."

Claire, though startled and thrilled, yet hesitated. "But won't she object? Her only child . . . and so sudden."

"God, no—she won't object," said Martin chuckling, "she's been after me to marry for ages, and she'll be so relieved that the bride isn't a damn Yankee! I'll phone her when we've eaten. You'll see."

They did scant justice to Claire's excellent Louisiana dinner, though Martin produced a treasured bottle of burgundy, and they toasted each other, smiling, both suffused by a glow which needed neither food nor drink for enhancement. As they finished with the special roast black coffee in demitasses, Claire was imbued with the joy that breeds universal good will and the wish to share it.

"Martin," she said, "you know it's poor little Amy who is really responsible for our finding each other. And you know?"

"What?" he said, running his fingers down the side

125

of her cheek. "I never realized what lovely bone struc-ture you have! Like that Praxiteles 'Aphrodite.' "

"Thanks, darling," she said turning her head and kissing his finger, "but my bone structure will last awhile, Amy needs *immediate* help, from what you tell me."

"Oh Lord." He sighed. "But I don't know how." And now *he* did not wish to be worried by Amy's problems.

"Let's take the Delatours to Louisiana for the wed-ding!" she exclaimed. "Amy needs a pleasant jolt, and I'd love to have her for my bridesmaid. I've so few friends or relations left down there."

"What, all *three* Delatours!" cried Martin laughing, and trying to examine the idea. "I must say there's plenty of room at Bellerive, and you can count on Mother's hospitality, but honestly, can you see *Sarah* on the Bayou Teche?" He thought of the lazy elegance of Bellerive. The black servants, some of whose fore-bears had once served Azilde's forebears—back and back into slavery days. He thought of the afternoons on the cool galéries, the mint juleps, the gentle gossip, the sumptuous meals lasting hours, the fragrance of gardenia and jasmine from the gardens which ran—near an avenue of the mysterious trailing gray of Span-ish moss—down to the old steamboat landing on the bayou. And he thought of his own mother, plumply voluptuous in the black velvets and laces she always wore, still in mourning for his father, as was the custom down there, and of the jeweled crucifix around her neck—the tapers she burned to the saints in St. Peter's Church. The vision of Sarah Mead Delatour, who might have posed for Grant Wood's famous grim-lipped puritanical farm wife, inhibited, bigoted, bony as a rake in her cheap nylon prints—

"No, my love," said Martin, "it's a charitable thought, but I won't have Sarah throwing our wedding into a deep freeze, and I can't see her letting Amy go without her. She hasn't changed *that* much. Besides, I'm not sure Amy would go if permitted—even with Grandpère. She's besotted over the Wilton youth."

"I know how the poor girl feels—besotted," said Claire with a rueful smile. "Nevertheless, the change might help, and if you're thinking of the fares . . ." she added timidly, "I've quite a bit saved, and . . ."

"Good Lord, sugar," he interrupted, pulling her around the little table onto his lap and shutting her up with a kiss. After a moment he continued, "I've enough for the fares though I want to spend a lot on a big splashy old-fashioned engagement ring—if you'd like that, of course," he added belatedly, realizing through the insight of this new tenderness, how dictatorial he had often been in his relations to women.

"Yes, I'd like anything. *I'm* in the dithering state of whatever thou wanteth, I want." She got off his lap and pushed him gently toward the living room. "Please, darling, phone your mother. I really do *so* hope that she approves. I guess I'm a pretty conventional type, after all."

For this remark Martin loved her even better. Generations of convention and of the ingrained chivalric attitude toward beloved women could not be erased by a few years of racketing around in the new permissive society.

Martin picked up the receiver and dialed New Iberia, Louisiana. Claire tactfully retired to the kitchen and shut the door. But there was no need for tact, Azilde after the first startled moments of listening to her son was genuinely delighted and asked to speak to Claire.

"Welcome, honey, to the family, and to Bellerive. I met your papa, the doctor, once or twice in N'yawlins when the Judge and I were livin' there, but ever'body knew about Dr. Colbert. Oh, this is the very nicest Christmas gift I evah did get! This big old house hasn't had a weddin' in it since my own." The warm drawl went on and on, happily oblivious to Martin's phone bill, thought Claire with amusement after she gave the phone back to Martin. Azilde had never counted pennies in her life. Some man had always cared for her finances; first, father, then husband, and now, Claire gathered, a Mr. Tournier, a lawyer-cousin in St. Martinville. A sweet, stressless life Azilde lived, but awfully soft; no wonder, perhaps, Martin had struck out on his own.

Martin at the telephone looked up at Claire once. "Mother wants to know if we have any northern guests we'd like to bring."

"Please tell her that it's possible," answered Claire, "three of them," and saw Martin's eyebrows raise, though he relayed the message.

When the phone call finally ended, he made a face at Claire and said, "If I weren't so much in love with you, I'd think you a stubborn little cuss. I thought we'd settled the Delatour question. I simply don't *want* any of that weird threesome at Bellerive. Actually, I wish to forget them for a while."

Claire inwardly flinched at the disapproval in his face, but she said staunchly, "We started to help Amy, and we haven't finished. Besides what you told me—I've a kind of premonition. I never used to have things like that, I still think they're dubious, but, Martin, if you start meddling with psyches, you *can't* suddenly lose interest, one has to persevere."

"That sounds very much like a criticism," he said sharply, reaching for his pipe and tamping down tobacco.

"And this," she said as lightly as she could, "sounds almost like the first quarrel." Her lips trembled and she swallowed hard.

He flung his pipe on the table. "We won't *let* it be! Blast the Delatours! Do as you wish, but come here to me, I much prefer kissing to arguing with a whim of iron."

Claire left for town on a late train, though it was very hard to leave him. She had a mass of work and preparations to surmount before going with Martin to Louisiana.

"I'll be out early Saturday morning," she assured him, "to help you tackle the Delatours, then I can stay until late Sunday."

"In your usual state of dogged purity?" he said chuckling. "My God, if it weren't for the way you kiss me, I'd think you frigid. I did begin to believe you found me repulsive—those nights here you made me sleep on the divan! You baffled me."

"Isn't anything worthwhile worth waiting for?" asked Claire softly. "And if it's any satisfaction to you, the super believes the worst. He gave me a distinct leer today—Oh, Martin," she added, suddenly serious, "I'm so *happy,* I guess I've loved you ever since our first dates at Tulane—though naturally I was too proud to show it."

Martin could not honestly say the same. His love had burst on him this very day, at least consciously, and all due to an outrageous lie he had told to protect himself and Amy. How bizarre, he thought—an ignoble action, not punished but gloriously rewarded. And Amy's problems would surely all be miraculously resolved, too, he felt buoyantly certain of this as he kissed Claire on the station platform and settled her in the train as though she were a fragile piece of porcelain.

But he was wrong. Amy's problems were not resolved.

When Claire came out to Greenwich on Saturday morning, after a blissful reunion with Martin, she phoned the Delatour flat, and got Sarah at once.

"I'm right glad to hear from you, Doctor," Sarah

said, her acid voice lowered almost to a whisper. "Was even thinking of calling Mr. Stone, since I don't know anyone else to help. Amy's gone queer again. Leastways, she's been shut up in her room since yesterday. Locked the door, won't come out, won't eat, and in the night I think I heard her crying. Even Mr. Delayter can't get at her."

"I'll be right over," said Claire slowly. She put down the receiver and stared at Martin, her arched brows drawn together in an anxious frown.

"Trouble," she said in answer to his questioning look, and told him Sarah's report. "I'll see what it's all about."

"I'll come with you," said Martin, sighing. He had planned a special day for them. First, inspect some quite beautiful engagement rings he had selected at the local jeweler's; then, lunch at an expensive topflight French country restaurant, while making honeymoon plans. A week in Jamaica? Barbados? If they got married on or about Christmas Day there would be enough time left before their respective classes, or they might both wangle a few extra days of vacation. Amy had receded, all his thoughts were now centered on Claire. And he almost resented—though part of him admired it—her continuing involvement with the girl.

"No, darling," said Claire, who understood him very well. "Don't come to the Delatours now, you'd be impatient, and I think this is a woman's job."

She kissed him and then walked briskly through the sparkling December cold up Steamboat Road, and Greenwich Avenue to the delicatessen, noting that the windows were full of Christmas tinsel, and hearing a poignant blare of carols from a radio.

In the Delatour flat there were no signs of approaching Christmas. Sarah did not hold with useless fripperies. The kitchen was, of course, immaculate, but it smelled of stale cooking and detergent.

Sarah and Pierre Delatour had been sitting silently at the table, until the former answered Claire's knock. "Silly to have bothered you," said Sarah gruffly, "and I'm sick and tired of Amy's carryings-on. She's been moony for weeks, like she wasn't really here, but you *said* to give her freedom, and what's come of *that?*" Sarah angrily waved a letter under Claire's nose. "School says she's not doing *any work*. That's what!"

Claire glanced at the letter from the high school, then at Amy's shut door.

"Can you make 'er come out?" asked the old man anxiously. *"Ma pauvre petite* Ange-Marie, she is un-'appy, she is 'ow you say? Like a wounded beast 'iding in its lair."

Claire concealed her own dismay. "I'll try," she said quietly. She looked at the two faces, one exasperated, one beseeching, though both showed deep concern. "Would you mind going out? There must be some errand," she spoke with the authority she had often had to use toward a worried family.

Sarah, immediately affronted, began indignant ex-postulation, but the old man rose at once and took Sarah's coat and his own from the corner coat rack.

"Come," he said to Sarah, *"venez!* Zis lady doctor maybe know best."

Claire waited in the kitchen until she could no longer hear Sarah's objections on the descending stairs. She took a deep breath and knocked on Amy's door. There was silence, until she heard the girl's muffled voice. "Oh, leave me *alone!*" It was a piteous wail, with an undertone of despair.

"It's Claire, dear—only Claire. Your mother and grandfather have gone out. I've come especially to see you. Please unlock the door."

Again Claire waited, willing that the girl would obey.

"I've a surprise for you," she said almost gaily. "A pleasant one. I can't tell you it through a *door*."

She thought she had failed, and began to envision grim measures—summoning the police, breaking in, force—no, better get Martin first, she *should* have let him come—when the key suddenly turned, the door was flung open, and Amy stood on the center of the hooked rug in her tiny room, her hands clenched, her head thrown back defiantly, but the look in her gray eyes was of stark suffering.

Claire advanced quickly and kissed her. "Now, what's all this?" she said matter-of-factly, holding the rigid little body close, and stroking the tangled chestnut hair.

"I'm no good—" whispered Amy through her teeth. "Mother says so, the school says so . . . and . . . and . . ."

Claire began to get an inkling and her heart sank. "Well, Martin and I don't think so," she said cheerfully, "and your grandfather doesn't. Nor does your mother, really." She drew the girl over to the cot and made her sit down close. "Any strange dreams lately?" she asked.

Amy shook her head, though she relaxed a little. "This happened in the *now*. Four days ago on Wednesday." Her voice was muffled against Claire's delicately scented blouse. "And then, after—and he doesn't even care enough to . . . to . . ." she gave a gulp, and began to tremble.

"*Who* doesn't? Mac Wilton?" breathed Claire, though she was certain. It was not hard to remember the anguish of rejected love at sixteen, nor, she thought, was it so different at twenty-seven, except that one had learned better methods of coping, the heart was not *totally* shattered. She lifted Amy's face and looked into the wild, frightened eyes. "Tell me, dear—" she said.

Amy twitched away, a dull red appeared in her pale

cheeks. "I'm no good!" she cried again. "Mother warned me—even Grandpère would despise me now —as *he* does, M-Mac." She began pleating and un-pleating a corner of her cheap blue bedspread. She was silent.

"I think I can guess," said Claire at last. "Let me help you talk. You and Mac . . ." she hesitated, searching for words which would not further evoke guilt, revulsion, or disturb Amy's extraordinary inno-cence. "You and Mac, well, something more intimate than you meant has happened—which is not the end of the world, Amy, and *has* been happening since the beginning of time. Why, I've treated dozens of other girls in your predicament, if *it is* one."

"I'm not dozens of other girls," cried Amy fiercely. "I'm different, I've always been."

That's true, for once, Claire thought. This poor child *is* unlike any I've known—but it was necessary to find out with a crudity she would not voice to Amy herself, how far things had actually gone.

"You had a date with Mac, Wednesday, I gather. Where did you go?"

Amy stopped pleating the bedspread, she turned from Claire and stared out of the window toward the parking lot. Just as Claire began to think that there would be no answer again, Amy spoke in a flat mono-tone.

"We went to Mac's home on Lake Avenue. His folks had all gone out for the evening. We sat in the den and watched TV awhile. Mac was drinking rum and Coke. I *asked* for one, Mac was always teasing me about my Puritan blood, he said I was hopelessly square, he'd like to see me liven up. The drink tasted good, I had another, then I felt fire in my veins. I used to be afraid of fire. I wasn't afraid of this, it was a sweet, warm fire. I wanted to melt in it when Mac kissed me. He'd never kissed me like that before. He said he loved me.

He tore open my dress—I wasn't even embarrassed. I *wanted* him to, I *wanted* more—can you understand *that?*"

"Perfectly," said Claire with a dry little laugh.

Amy was not listening, she went on in the same dead voice. "Later Mac took me home, he didn't say much, but I didn't either, I lay here on this cot all night, so keyed up, still feeling that fire in my veins. But next day at school, Mac didn't come near me. He didn't come to the Student Center for lunch block. I'd see him in the distance. I couldn't understand it, we'd been making plans for the weekend, and I thought I'd see him a lot during the Christmas vacation. Thursday night he phoned me here. He sounded mean and strange. He said he had to go to New York this week-end with his parents, and that he was afraid he wouldn't be here for the vacation, he was going skiing in Vermont at Peggy Manson's ski lodge—he knew I couldn't ski. He'd see me around after New Year's maybe."

Amy stopped. She began again on the bedspread, pleating and unpleating the corner. Her eyes were dry, but Claire's were not.

"I told you I was no good," said Amy.

"Nonsense!" Claire exploded furiously, wishing she could strangle Mac Wilton with her bare hands, "and though I don't suppose anybody likes to hear of other people's happiness when they're miserable, I wish you to share mine. Martin and I are being married at Christmas in Louisiana, you and your family are invited, and I ask *you* to be my bridesmaid."

It took Amy a moment to understand, then the woefulness turned puzzled. "Louisiana wedding? And you want *me?*"

"More than anything in the world—except Martin," answered Claire. "I came here today to invite you all to my wedding, and now I see how important the trip will be to keep you from moping during the vacation."

"Mother'd *never*—" whispered Amy. "I'm trapped —trapped," she repeated, turning from Claire. "No way out."

"You're not!" cried Claire vehemently. She had heard those hopeless words from youngsters who attempted suicide. "You're strong, Amy. Your Acadian blood, your Yankee blood, both come from strong, brave people. The first Ange-Marie was strong to endure." She saw that the girl heard her, the dangerous desperation slowly left her eyes, now she merely looked forlorn.

Claire spoke in sharp command, "I want you to eat something, and try to behave normally until everything's settled. I know you're suffering, and I understand it, but your mother and Mr. Delatour have also suffered about *you*. Think of *them*, too, dear."

When Amy was apathetically drinking milk, Claire let herself out of the drab flat, and just managed to miss the returning Delatours. She was in no mood to be questioned, and fairly certain that, temporarily relieved by confession, Amy *would* act normal, but Claire's own anger grew until it exploded again in Martin's apartment. "My God, what a callous bastard!" she cried of Mac, after she had told Amy's story. "I'd like to *murder* him!" She began to pace the shag rug.

"Whoa, sugar!" said Martin, laughing a little. "I didn't know I'd got me such a wildcat. Where's my calm, unflappable Claire? Though indignation for someone else is most becoming."

She was not listening. "He ought to be horse-whipped, seducing her, then giving her the brush-off like that, Amy's not strong enough to take it, I'm afraid for her, and gosh, she may be pregnant, and that *would* ruin her, so much guilt already, and . . ."

"Sit *down*, quietly," said Martin. "Listen to me and stop sputtering." He waited until Claire collapsed on the divan and lit a cigarette. "Now, first—" he went on, "I've seen a fair amount of Mac, I know his record, I think he's a decent guy. In the second place Amy seems to have asked for it, but I think there's an explanation. At least, I mean to find out, though it's not a job I relish."

"You'll talk to Mac?" she looked up at him hopefully, then made a discouraged sound. "What good'd *that* do? We know the facts, and males having had their will, *do* get suddenly bored, though it's beastly."

"I detect—" said Martin, "in that pessimistic speech, not only echoes of the Victorian era, but overtones of Women's Lib. Men aren't *all* heels, Claire."

"No," she said, her anger fading. "Of course not. It's just that Amy is so vulnerable—and I'm very fond of her. Besides, you *can't* talk to Mac today. He told Amy he would be in New York."

"I doubt it," said Martin dryly. "Anyway, I'll track him down. I don't want the entire weekend ruined for *us.*"

Mac was not in New York, he was at his home with some of his friends, preparing to watch an afternoon sports program on TV. "I won't keep you long," said Martin on the phone, "but I want to talk to you on a matter of great importance."

"What about, Mr. Stone?" Mac sounded angry and defensive.

"Not on the phone, but it's urgent. I'll be at Boodle's in ten minutes, and expect to meet you there."

"OK," said the boyish voice sulkily, after a minute.

Boodles was the restaurant and bar in high favor just now with young people. It was also about midway between Mac's house and Martin's apartment. Neutral ground.

Martin got there first and ordered two beers. He was relieved when he saw the handsome, frowning face above huge shoulders in a leather jacket. Martin stood up and signaled.

"I don't get this," said Mac, glancing around at the nearly empty bar, but accepting the beer. "What's there to talk about?"

"Amy Delatour," said Martin.

Mac's mouth tightened. "Any business of *yours?*"

"Yes," said Martin, "of mine and my fiancée, Claire Colbert. We're being married at Christmas in Louisiana. We're taking Amy with us, I hope. You're giving that girl an awfully rough time, Mac, but I'm not here to moralize, I want bare facts."

The boy's frown cleared somewhat. He took a long swig of beer. "Such as?" he said more amiably. "I don't want to hurt the girl, but I think she's nuts. I did like her a lot."

"Has it occurred to you that she might be pregnant?" asked Martin quietly, "and *that,* even in this day and age, is a mess."

Mac flushed. Despite Boodle's tactful gloom, one could see the dark blood rise. "Not by *me* she isn't pregnant," said Mac grimly. "No way. I guess I shouldn't have let her have those drinks, and we both got worked up and how she acted, I was sure it wasn't the first time for her. I don't say it wasn't a near miss —but she turned me off."

"How so?" asked Martin.

"Because she called me 'Paul' twice. She jabbered about fire in her veins, she got sort of wild, her voice changed, got deeper, and then she began speaking French. Floods of French. She acted like I *was* 'Paul,' and I didn't like it. I got turned off. I'm not going to make it—make love to any girl who doesn't even remember my name, or who she's with."

"I see . . ." said Martin after a pause. "I don't know as I blame you. I can only explain that Amy has a psychological problem, and she hasn't been involved with any Paul, and if you'd gone on, it *would* have been the first time for her. You'll have to believe me. She isn't technically nuts, though she doesn't *know* what she said to you."

Mac looked unconvinced, yet perturbed.

They both stood up. "I guess there's nothing more," said Martin, "thanks for explaining, it's relieved my mind in one way."

They walked together toward the door, as they parted Mac spoke gruffly. "Don't get me wrong, Mr. Stone. I *like* Amy, I like her a lot. I know she liked me, but there's something screwy, I guess it scared me." He gave a sheepish grin. "She's really a damn sweet kid."

"OK, Mac, I understand how it was."

Claire had been sitting impatiently by Martin's big window, watching the first drift of snowflakes fall on the harbor; she turned as he came in. *"That* didn't take long," she said. "Didn't you see Mac?"

"Sure"—he filled his pipe and smiled at her—"and he has an explanation which I totally believe. First, Amy's *not* pregnant, since they never really got to first base. Second, she 'turned him off' to use his own repeated phrase."

"How? She's mad about him."

"After the drinks took hold, the sexual 'fire in her veins' apparently threw her back into the Nova Scotian life, and her great love then. She kept calling poor Mac, 'Paul' and she reverted to vehement French. She seems to have frightened Mac, as well as making him think she'd been messing around with some Paul."

"I see," said Claire after a moment. "Yes, fear and love, the most dynamic emotions, strong enough to carry over—transcend the barrier. We conquered the fear for Amy, or *she* did, with our help, but the second —the passionate love she bore Paul, the waiting, the yearning—the fierce joy of complete union at last—

and of course that thing with Mac is the first sexual encounter in *this* life. It made the link."

Martin quirked his eyebrows. "So you've really come around to the reincarnation theory?"

"Not certain," said Claire frowning. "I suppose that in some mysterious way, this *could* be genetic memory, the Acadian Ange-Marie was Amy's ancestress—but the point is, what do we do now? On one level it would relieve Amy's dreadful hurt if we told her the truth. On the other hand I think it would be dangerous for her to think she is even more abnormal than she suspects. Martin"—she looked up at him tenderly—"could you use hypnosis just *once* more? This time not from scientific curiosity, but to help calm and reassure her. Her unconscious will accept, I hope, what the conscious mind can't face."

Chapter Seven

On Saturday, December 22, on a Delta plane bound for New Orleans, Amy sat by the window in tourist class section next to her grandfather, immediately behind Martin and Claire.

Amy had been momentarily interested in the take-off, and now by the stupendous view of limitless blue sky with a bank of clouds beneath them, though the real Amy still seemed to be veiled away from the outside world. She was not nearly as thrilled as Grandpère, who kept craning over her to see, and making excited comments in French. *"Incroyable . . . ! Magnifique!"*

Grandpère's eyes were bright, his cheeks ruddy above the neatly trimmed beard. He wore his only good suit, a black one, bought long ago in Rivière du Loup, and last worn for the funerals of his son, Louis, and then his grandson, Amy's brother. The association did not disturb him. Those griefs were long past, and after all, death happened to everyone, and must be accepted, as one accepted the leafless trees, and the snows of winter, secure in the certainty of renewed spring at last. In this world, or the next, according to God's will. He had, however, dipped into his tiny savings, which he hid under a board in his shop—as his forefathers had hid theirs. The savings were destined for Amy, in time, but he had decided that a new striped shirt and a bright magenta tie would please her more right now. He constantly thought of things which might cheer Amy, saddened that she no longer was close to him, nor laughed and joked in private, as she used to. Besides, he did not want Amy or the charming young couple who had made this trip possible to be ashamed of his appearance. One should observe *"les convenances,"* thought Grandpère, happily accepting a beer from the pretty stewardess, and glad that his daughter-in-law had not wished to go South.

Martin and Claire also rejoiced that Sarah had not come. "No junketings around the country for *me,*" she said when Claire first broached the subject. "You couldn't get me in one of those aereoplanes for love nor money, besides, I'm tuckered out, and my cousins'll be glad to have me. Amy can go with Mr. Delayter since you and Mr. Stone are kind enough to invite 'em. Frankly, Doctor, I'll be glad of a rest; my leg hurts and I've been more worried about Amy than I let on."

"I know," Claire had said with sympathy, "but she's been OK this week, hasn't she?" Martin's hypnosis seemed to work well. He had calmed, reassured, then given a very strong post-hypnotic suggestion that during the last few days Amy would ignore Mac Wilton, scarcely realize that he was at school, that she could concentrate on the trip to Louisiana, and not worry about anything.

"Dunno," said Sarah slowly. "Oh, she hasn't done anything wild again, like locking herself in her room, but she acts beat. . . . That Wilton boy throw her over?" she added crisply.

Claire's startled silence was assent enough. She had not expected that much insight.

"I got jilted once," said Sarah, " 'twasn't pleasant, but I held my head high and showed some spunk, though I don't say that if I'd had the chance to get clear away for a while, like Amy's doing, I mightn't 've taken it." Before Claire—who was touched by this confidence—could speak, Sarah had reverted to her usual tartness. "But why that Mr. Delayter, the old fool, wants to go off gallivanting at his age, and with his bad heart—crazy."

Claire had said quietly that he was well supplied with nitroglycerine tablets, and his doctor had sanctioned the trip.

Sarah snorted—and that was the end of the interview. So here they were, winging South, winging home through the heavenly blue skies to happiness, thought Claire, amused at her own sentimental phraseology. Under cover of the morning paper, her hand reached for and found Martin's.

His hand enfolded hers so tightly that it crushed the big diamond engagement ring into her finger. They sat that way until the lunch snacks were served.

The plane landed on time at the New Orleans airport. Azilde had sent Old Ben, the middle-aged chauffeur-handyman, to meet them in the ancient but gleaming dark blue Cadillac, which was part of Martin's boyhood memories. Azilde used it seldom, and had seen no reason for buying a new one.

Ben, his chocolate-brown face beaming, pumped Martin's hand, then Claire's. "Welcome home, Mistah Martin," he cried. "Yo' Ma's powerful excited, she'd a come too, only she was tired after fussin' all day in the kitchen, stirrin' Chris'mus cake with Cindy, an' beatin' the biscuits her own se'f, like she allus does. Mighty purty bride yo' got, Mistah Martin," added Ben, showing his white teeth in a dazzling smile. His kindly eyes rested on the Delatours. "These the no'thern weddin' guests?"

"Yes, Ben," said Martin, laughing. He had forgotten Ben's curiosity, his garrulousness, and his involvement with the family, of which he was totally a part—something they didn't understand up North. "This is Mr. Pierre Delatour and his granddaughter."

"Pleased to meet you folks," said Ben, shaking their hands. "Delatour, you say? There's a family o' Cajuns called Delatour, up the road a piece from Bellerive —nearer Ma'tinville."

"Oh?" said Martin, startled. He had been raised in New Orleans, spending only holidays and an occasional summer month at Bellerive, and had never really much explored the Bayou Teche country. It was only since his father's death that Azilde had moved permanently back to her old home.

Pierre did not understand what Ben had said in the strange drawling accent, and was furthermore dazzled by the novelty of this adventure—the smells, the warm breeze, the flickering lights, the long blue Cadillac awaiting them.

But Amy understood, and her dazed apathy was punctured. "Delatours . . . ?" she whispered, "and the black man pronounced it *right*. How funny."

Nobody heard her for Martin swooped Claire under his arm, stowed her in the front seat, and cried exuberantly, "I'll drive, Ben—you get in back with the others. Gosh, it's good to be home, and under *these* circumstances!" He gave Claire's knee a squeeze, then put the car in gear.

The December daylight changed abruptly to night as they sped west along U.S. 90, bound for New Iberia, 140 miles away. There was little to see between towns, only the dark, mysterious flatness of cypress swamps, with here and there a gleam of water. None of them spoke much, except Ben, who was trying to entertain the northern guests, and proffered tidbits of information—the annual blessing of the shrimp fleet, the trapping of muskrats, the growing of sugar cane—with a sigh for the old days when the Lavals of Bellerive had been one of the greatest sugar planters in the county, rice, too—now there wasn't hardly nothin' left of the ol' plantation, but Judge Stone, he'd been right smart, he'd put money into them oil refineries, across the Teche from Jeannerette. "It's a mercy yo' cain't see them great stinkin' fiery blasts from Bellerive," said Ben. "Ol' Missy—that's Miz Stone—she don't like change, nor does us'n. Cindy an' me, she's ma wife, nor Ramon, he's the butler, been at Bellerive so long, he served crawfish an' gumbo in the big house 'fore my Ol' Missy was even born. We allus been happy at Bellerive—that means 'Beautiful River Bank' in French. Ain't so sure about Shirley, though, does the chamber work, uppity piece from Lafayette, allus grumblin' she wants to go No'th, lazy as a 'gator in the sun. We ain't had her long, and Ol' Missy, she ought to fire her, 'cep' she hate to make fusses, she'm so kind-hearted."

Claire listened to some of this with half an ear, while she sat snuggled close to Martin. "Your mother certainly inspires loyalty," she said. "Oh, I can't *wait* to get there!" she added with a girlish catch in her voice.

Martin laughed. "Pretty soon, my love—see those red flames way ahead against the sky? The refineries at Jeannerette—and just think—how long do you guess this trip took a hundred years ago? Three, four days, that's what. They had to go all around and down the bayous on steamboats, hoping to find channels that weren't silted up. Even the train, when they *finally* got a railroad, took a day or more. Before steamboats they used pirogues and portages, must have taken a month, and yet St. Martinville, quite near Bellerive, was called 'Petit Paris,' with balls and its own opera house, after some of the French noblemen escaped the guillotine in *their* Revolution and settled way out here. I'm not quite sure why they picked the Bayou Teche, but my de Laval ancestor was among them. Santiagos were Spanish, they came earlier and then married Lavals. Mother's a real Creole, pure French and Spanish blood, and very proud of it."

"That's romantic," said Claire sincerely, amused at his teacher's zest for imparting facts, and fascinated by the long-established lineage she was about to join. Her own Colberts, though French way back, had been shopkeepers in New Orleans, until her father came along and studied medicine. As for her mother, she had been only one generation removed from Hamburg.

Martin crossed the Teche, skirted the industrial part of New Iberia, with some help from Ben at the turns, speeded north along the river road, and gave a grunt of satisfaction as he saw a picket fence and two white gateposts on the right. He swung the car into a graveled drive which ran for over a mile up an avenue of live oaks festooned with trailing Spanish moss, long enough in places to brush the car top. The headlights illumined the eerie beauty of the hanging gray moss.

Amy, on the back seat, leaned forward and spoke so suddenly that Martin and Claire both jumped. *"That's* what Longfellow thought he meant," said the girl in a clear, critical voice. " 'The murmuring pines and the hemlocks . . . bearded with moss . . . stand like harpers hoar, with beards that rest on their bosoms.' *Pines* and *hemlocks* don't have beards. They didn't have in Nova Scotia, either. I *said* he was all mixed up."

"So you did," answered Martin, glad that the girl had broken her long silences with a spontaneous remark, yet somewhat disturbed. He and Claire thought Amy cured of her compulsive interest in that poem, and all its melancholy evocation of the far past.

"We're almost in this *southern* Evangeline country," he added slowly. "We might show you tomorrow, if you want, and I suspect you'll feel a lot of inaccuracies, but they hardly matter, it is really the concept that

145

matters of tragic, patient fidelity—that is what has made the story endure—Evangeline's practically a saint down here—" he broke off as he saw the great plantation house ahead, its many windows sparkling with lighted candles, the front door open wide behind the six white Doric columns. In the doorway, silhouetted against the light, stood a tall black figure with its arms outstretched.

He stopped the car, and ran toward the woman in black.

Claire had a lump in her throat as she watched the reunion of mother and son, and heard through the car window the sound of happy weeping and broken murmurs. A quiver of jealousy constricted her throat for she saw the warmth of Martin's hug, and the way he bent to kiss her. The feeling passed when Azilde disengaged herself and came down the steps to the car, crying in a voice of great sweetness. "Claire? Let me see you, honey—wheah's my Martin's bride?"

Then Claire was enfolded against a black velvet bosom scented with jasmine, and drawn into the house followed by a smiling Martin.

Ramon, the butler, stood bowing by the door; he held an ornate silver tray bearing little silver cups of eggnog. He was old and lean, his creased black skin had a bluish cast, his features were as austere as Ben's were jolly, his ancestors had come into the family with the Santiagos two hundred years ago; he was proud of that, and of the Spanish Christian name he bore, but he was no less devoted to Azilde than Ben was.

Azilde, still bubbling with welcome, started to offer the first ceremonial eggnog to Claire, when she caught herself with a cry of contrition. "I decleah, Martin, I've forgotten your guests. That's dreadful. Where *are* they?"

Claire and Martin, too, had forgotten, but Ben had not. They were waiting in the doorway.

"Mistah and Miss Delatour," said Ben importantly, shooing them into the great central hall. "They've had a long journey, fust plane trip, too. I 'spect they're famished."

"But o' *course!*" cried Azilde. Her large smiling black eyes surveyed the pair, and if she was surprised to see, as the very special northern guests, a chunky old man in a rusty black suit with a hideous tie, and a tight-lipped uneasy little girl who scuffed her feet, no hint of anything but cordiality showed on Azilde's lovely creamy-skinned face.

The Delatours sipped at the eggnog, but even Grandpère was speechless. He had never imagined such a place as this. Four great rooms opened off on either side of the central hall. There was a pungent smell of cypress and pine from the four unnecessary fires. *He* thought the night very warm. He had glimpses of Aubusson rugs, of gilt and crystal candelabra, of ormulu tables, of tapestried chairs, and scenic wallpaper behind portraits—dozens of portraits of people in what looked like costumes to him. Then there were flowers, more flowers than at the mayor of Rivière du Loup's funeral. Dishes of velvety pink ones with waxy green leaves, flowers with strange shapes, some like a bird's head, and silvery foliage in a dozen china vases stuck everywhere in corners, on tables, in a lavish profusion that made him uncomfortable. He could not understand such wasteful luxury, and a shade of amazed disapproval showed in his eyes.

"Ah . . ." said Azilde, noting this, and ever careful to please any guest, "you must be tired, Mr. Delatour —all of you will want to freshen up befoah dinner, I'll show you the rooms."

"Zank you, madame," said Pierre with dignity, "ze voyage was much, *peut-être.*"

Azilde smiled, "Oh, yes, Martin told me you are French, from Canada, *nous pouvons parler français ensemble,* my maman always spoke French to me, and then in the convent, but I've forgotten a lot."

The old man got only the gist of this, since her French phrase was not pronounced quite as he would have—though Amy understood. She had learned a Parisian accent at high school—of which place she did not wish to be reminded. And the unexpected luxury of Bellerive disquieted her as much as it did Grandpère; she felt alien, rootless. She knew that her hostess was charming, but Azilde was also overpowering in her black velvet dress with black lace sleeves, the multi-jeweled crucifix sparkling on the lush rounded bosom, and bracelets which glittered, and rings—diamonds, surely, on the very white tapering fingers. She felt Claire looking at her anxiously, and tried to smile, but Claire, too, had receded into the shimmering opulence. Moreover, Claire now wore a big square-cut diamond on *her* hand. She would soon be part of all this herself.

I wish we hadn't come, Amy thought, and was at once checked by the dismal awareness that the little flat in Greenwich would have been no happier. I don't belong anywhere, she thought. She was further daunted by her bedroom, when Azilde ushered her in and turned on the light. It seemed as big as a skating rink. Dozens of velvety scatter rugs on the gleaming mahogany floors, armchairs, a desk with crystal fittings, the enormous four-poster bed of carved rosewood, with embroidered tester, and mosquito netting neatly festooned out of the way for winter.

And her bathroom! So many mirrors! And the dazzle of porcelain with a violet pattern, and *gold* taps shaped like dolphins. A violet rug, amber bath salts, pink soap, rosy towels with a gilt monogram, and scented *blue water* in the toilet bowl! Amy stared around with her mouth open. Then she stared at herself in one of the full-length mirrors, and slowly shriveled. She looked diminished, rumpled, her hair was stringy, her glasses made her look like a bulgy-eyed toad, she had a spot coming on her chin. I'm ugly, she thought, *ugly*. No wonder Mac . . . wouldn't . . . didn't . . .

The tenuous barrier erected by Martin in hypnosis —aided by her own deepest self-protective instincts— suddenly collapsed. Suffocating waters of total rejection and abandonment engulfed her.

She gasped, holding her hands tight clenched on her chest. She turned blindly, stumbling out of that mirrored bathroom and flung herself crosswise on the embroidered counterpane of the huge four-poster bed, her head buried in her arms.

Downstairs in the north drawing room, Azilde, Martin and Claire waited. The ladies had sherry in silver-gilt goblets, Martin drank Bourbon, while Ramon passed Azilde's tiny beaten biscuits loaded with a pâté made from a secret recipe which had come down through the centuries in Azilde's family.

At first they chatted animatedly of the wedding plans. There had been a slight hitch, Azilde explained apologetically. The twenty-seventh was the earliest date to receive the bishop's dispensation, and the earliest that St. Peter's priest was free to solemnize the ceremony in his rectory parlor. "Mixed marriage . . ." said Azilde, sighing, then instantly smiled reassuringly at Claire. "O' course, *I* had one, too, my parents were horrified, devastated—I didn't care—I *loved* David Livingston Stone, he wasn't judge *then,* and such a happy marriage. O' course, he *was* from Loosiana, too, even though American."

Claire met Martin's eyes. In the excitement of their own new love, they had not talked about religion. She had vaguely realized that he was baptized a Catholic. And so, I suppose, my children will have to be, she knew that much about the faith, and the fact was unimportant. The shadowy children they might have some day—neither they, nor anything else impinged on her quiet rapture. She telegraphed this in answer to Martin's questioning, slightly anxious look, and smiled back at Azilde. "It's so good of you to give the wedding in this fairy-tale place, please don't take much trouble, we just want . . ."

"To get married," said Martin, laughing, "and your new daughter-in-law is a pillar of respectability." He winked at his mother. "You really didn't have to stick me out in the *garçonnière,* honey," he said, referring to a small octagonal cottage adjacent to the house. "Claire and I would be entirely good and proper under the same roof!"

"O' course," said Azilde, looking a trifle perplexed. She had no knowledge of the laxness now prevalent in the outside world. "But bachelors *always* slept in the *garçonnière,* especially if they have a fiancée in the big house. It's the custom. Your papa slept there before we married. I had it specially aired and fixed up for you, isn't it all right?"

Martin laughed. "It's exquisite, like everything you arrange. I was teasing you." He blew her a kiss, and she responded with an instinctively coquettish lift of her chin, while her black eyes rested on him adoringly. Her big, lanky blond son, he resembled his father, yet his temperament—ah, much of that came from the Lavals. Such a sorrow it had been that she had never been able to bear another child, despite the prayers, the candles to Our Lady. Though soon, there might be grandchildren, she had prayed for that, too. She gave Claire a warm, approving glance.

"Look here—" said Martin, suddenly glancing at the French clock on the marble mantel, "it's after eight —aren't the Delatours taking a very long time upstairs?"

"Perhaps a little nap?" suggested Azilde comfortingly, time was unimportant to her. "You said the old gentleman had been ill. Maybe the girl was tired, too, she looked pale."

Claire was jolted into realization that she had again forgotten the Delatours, and felt a pang of apprehension, though Martin accepted his mother's comment. "As a matter of fact, they've both been ill—in a way," he said. "You must wonder why we brought them, but too complicated to explain, and I knew I could trust your hospitality—that reminds me, Ben said there were some Delatours up the road toward St. Martinville, do you happen to know?"

Azilde frowned slightly. "I think I've heard of them —oh yes, they raised chickens. Mama used to buy pullets from them when we had a special party. Those Delatours were *Cajuns*, o' course."

Azilde's faint distaste as she said "Cajuns" was apparent to both Martin and Claire. They recognized the ingrained prejudice once felt by all the aristocratic Creoles toward the tough, insular French peasants who had settled many of the bayous, as they infiltrated Louisiana some years after the Great Expulsion in Nova Scotia.

"Don't be snooty, dear," said Martin lightly. "Your guests upstairs come from Acadian stock in Canada, from which the name was contracted here to 'Cajun,' they are a remarkable people who suffered much, worked very hard, French-speaking, and as Catholic as you are, besides many of them have risen high in the government here, outstanding."

Azilde looked unconvinced. "I suppose so," she said doubtfully. "We just never had anything to do with them. Mama and Papa always thought it was silly when we had Yankee guests who wanted to go see that statue of Evangeline—some *movie actress* posed for it, I remembah."

Again Claire and Martin exchanged glances of amused tolerance. Azilde was as she was, and must be so accepted. Martin abandoned any attempt at instruction or the surmounting of antiquated class barriers. "Our guests upstairs bring one sure bid for your *compassion,* anyway," he said. "Mr. Delatour has a bad heart, physically—while Amy is suffering from heartbreak, emotionally, which is probably more painful."

Azilde put down her sherry, and stared at her son. "That child has been crossed in love?" she asked incredulously. "Poah little thing. We must try to distract her. There's the de Lauriaux near Lafayette, very good family, they have a son, he's charming, so gallant, beautiful manners, about twenty, I should think. I've asked them to the wedding, but we might arrange something earlier, we'll dress her up real pretty, I've got boxes of lovely old dresses in the attic. Shirley can make them fit. She is a grumpy, restless little Nigra, she's real ornery, but she likes to sew. Cindy and I'll teach her yet to behave herself. She needs a firm hand, that's all, I know how to train them."

Claire almost laughed at this complacent speech, thinking of the resentment, the incomprehension it would rouse among the blacks in the Harlem ghetto where she worked as a volunteer. But there was something more immediate than racial tangles. "Excuse me, Mrs. Stone," she said, rising, "I think I must just check on the Delatours."

Claire ran up the winding mahogany staircase to the bedrooms. She knocked at Pierre's door first, and heard him say, *"Entrez."*

He was standing somewhat shakily by the pier glass adjusting his lurid magenta tie. "I 'ope zey do not wait too much—" he said apologetically. "I lie down, I 'ad a leetle pain, I tak' my pill, I sleep a leetle—"

"It's all right," said Claire, patting his shoulder and picking off a thread of lint. "Do you feel like going

152

down now?" As he nodded, she added, "Have you seen Amy?"

He shook his head, frowning. "Zis enormous place —lak museum I visit once in New York, she mebbe lost . . . ?"

Claire frowned and went down the broad carpeted corridor past many doors of empty rooms, until behind one she heard the sounds she had been unconsciously dreading. Muffled mewing sounds, like an animal in pain, interspersed with rending sobs.

"Oh, God," Claire thought as they threw open the door and saw a crumpled-up body lying on the huge bed. *Now* what's happened! Lord, we should never have brought her. How bad is *this* break?

For once at a complete loss, Claire watched the shuddering figure in the wrinkled red pantsuit, which looked like a blood stain on the white bedspread. Pierre, equally distressed, cried, "Ange-Marie!" in an imploring voice, but the girl continued to make pitiful mewing sounds.

They were staring helplessly at the bed when Azilde came up behind them and pushed past them. "I wondered what was wrong," she said with composure. "Martin sent me up." She examined Amy. "Poah little one. Mama used to call this kind of thing the vapors. I had them once when I was in my teens, my sister, too. That's right, honey—" she added to the back of Amy's head, "cry it out! That's best! Claire, there's smellin' salts in the bathroom, will you get them?"

Claire started, then obeyed, relieved by the casual reception of Amy's condition, by the voice, however gentle and drawling, of a woman who perfectly understood love-sick emotions and even hysteria of this kind.

But Azilde did not know the whole story, she did not know Amy's dangerous psychic states, she did not know

153

the anxieties Pierre Delatour, Martin, and Claire had all repeatedly felt about this girl.

And far better that Azilde didn't know, Claire realized, as she drew back against the wall with the old man, and watched Amy gradually respond to Azilde's practical ministrations. "Hold yoah head up, sugah, and sniff this." Amy sniffed the smelling salts and choked. "That's good," said Azilde. "Now, do it again." Amy did so, and sneezed violently.

"That's *very* good," said Azilde. "That's all the bad hurty things burstin' out o' you. Now get up, come with me to the bathroom. We'll wash your face, rub cologne on your wrists." She put her arm around the girl and drew her unresisting to the bathroom, doused a washcloth with cold water, and scrubbed Amy's face. "Feel better?" she asked.

Amy drew a quivering sigh, looking up at the kind maternal eyes which regarded her with detached sympathy. "I—I guess so," she said, then gave a little chuckle which sounded to Grandpère, at least, like the normal Amy of last summer. "You know, Mrs. Stone," she said, "it's silly, but this bathroom frightened me, I've never seen anything like it. And then the mirrors —mirrors—" she paused, frowning, why had the mirrors frightened her?

Azilde paid no attention, she went on chafing Amy's wrists and neck with cologne, but Claire, who knew the girl so well, had an intuition. Amy, projected into a completely foreign environment, had been revolted by the Amy she thought she saw in the mirrors. Her shaky self-esteem had given way, shattered for a while, yet she seemed to have recovered, she began to look more natural.

"Now," said Azilde, quite briskly, "high time to eat. Cindy'll be fussin' that her gumbo's burned, and her meringues' fallen. But first, when we get down, you must both"—she gave Pierre Delatour a cordial smile

154

—"have a tot of brandy. That'll set you up." Amy smiled a little, and came with them, to Claire's great relief.

The next day was Sunday, and Martin drove them in the Cadillac to Mass at St. Peter's Church in New Iberia. Ben followed in the plantation truck with the other servants. Everybody always went to Mass from Bellerive. Pierre Delatour was delighted to go and take Amy, who—*la pauvre enfant*—had never had any religious instruction, except a few weeks at Greenwich's Congregational Sunday school, which did not count. Of late years he had skipped Mass himself, being tired on Sundays, and no longer strong enough to combat Sarah's outspoken disapproval. The thought that soon he must return to the squalid rooms over the delicatessen and that sour woman made him unhappy, though he was not easy at Bellerive either, thankful as he was to its hospitable mistress. She had been good to Amy last night, she was Catholic, she was part French, but she was *"une grande dame,"* and he felt an immense gulf between them. His grandmother used to tell him tales she had heard of the old days in France, before they all left Normandy, of the lord of the manor for whom those far-past Delatours farmed the land, as serfs. Very haughty he was, that seigneur, cruel, too, a Delatour had had his ears and nose cut off for poaching one pheasant from the seigneur's preserve. The seigneur's wife, la comtesse, might have been kind enough, since Pierre remembered hearing that she had sent swaddling clothes and three sous to every peasant woman who delivered a healthy child. But what of that? had said his grandmother, shrugging, the gifts were only to celebrate the arrival of another pair of hands to work—eventually—for the seigneur. Perhaps Azilde de Laval Stone was not so arrogant, yet he saw clearly that she stemmed from the same breed as that eighteenth-century aristocrat, and with some justification —though Azilde herself did not know it—he felt in her a tinge of benevolent condescension.

Amy's outburst last night had indeed done her good, as Azilde predicted. At least she was no longer dazed and numb. She enjoyed the Mass. There was a far-off familiarity about the priest in his violet chasuble, the burning tapers on the elaborate altar, the saints' statues, the kneeling congregation, the ringing of the sanctuary bell, and the French parts of the bi-lingual sermon. All these felt *right* and comfortable, as the luxury of Bellerive did not. Moreover, a natural youthful zest for novelty produced interest in the strange landscape as they drove home.

She stared at the Spanish moss as it waved gently in a warm breeze from the Gulf of Mexico. She exclaimed over the black cypress stumps in the swamps, and was aghast when Martin showed her an alligator, slithering into the bayou.

Later, at the magnificent dinner, ceremoniously served by Ramon, Amy encountered many tastes for the first time. The scalloped oysters she simply could not chew. Some of the dishes included the native Tabasco which burned her tongue and spoiled for her, as they did for her grandfather, many of the unheard of delicacies—crab soup, suckling pig, wild duck. The wines which accompanied each course she sipped at politely and thought them awfully vinegary. But the *desserts* entranced her, especially meringues loaded with chilled chocolate mousse, and the pecan pie.

"Oh, these are so *good!*" she cried with childish enthusiasm, accepting her third meringue. "Mrs. Stone, I never knew there was food like this in the whole wide world!"

Azilde smiled, well pleased, though entirely unable to imagine Amy's usual fare of stew, TV dinners, and an occasional hot dog.

Claire whispered to Martin in a relieved aside, "Amy's certainly acting like a normal girl, at last I believe she's really pulling out of it."

Martin said, "Uh-huh, seems so." He frowned a little, remembering his chance encounter with Mac Wilton in the glass corridor the last day of school. Mac had been embarrassed, offhand. "Hope you have a nice Christmas, Mr. Stone—Amy doing OK? Been too busy to see her—aw—you understand."

Martin had nodded. The boy continued quickly, "She really going with you to Louisiana? One of the kids said you had a plantation down there."

"Yes, my mother's—at New Iberia on the Bayou Teche, which practically nobody up here has ever heard of." Martin had laughed, a little puzzled by Mac's expression, as though he wanted to say something more, and didn't know how. "And *you*," said Martin, "will be merrily skiing in Vermont—have a good time."

"Sure," said Mac, "I'm crazy about skiing, and there's a great crowd going. I can't wait." And still for a moment he hung around dangling his guitar by the strap— he had just finished playing Christmas carols in the gym with the school combo. "Well—so long," said Mac abruptly, "be seeing you next year!" And hurried off.

Martin had not mentioned so trivial an incident to Claire, in fact he had forgotten it, and forgot it now again, as Claire leaned against his shoulder. "You going to show me the gardens, honey?" she whispered. "I don't mean to be shameless, but we haven't been alone together since we got here."

He smiled down at her. "There's an old marble bench near the bayou, very secluded, and we'll be as shameless as you'll let me, my virtuous one."

At three, the two elders went upstairs to rest. Azilde for her usual siesta, and Pierre Delatour, because he

157

was inordinately tired, though he felt guilty—there should be something that needed doing, at home there was always a leaky faucet, a loose hinge, a frayed electric cord for him to repair on a Sunday afternoon. Here all was languor and aimlessness. And so strangely hot for December. Hard to breathe. Yet he, too, was relieved about his little Ange-Marie, comforted that she had taken his arm in the old confiding way, before he went upstairs, had really smiled at him and shown all the perception she used to show when she murmured, "You don't much like it here, Grandpère, do you?"

"Non," he answered her in French, "I am like a stupid old frog, drowning in cream. *Déplacé, toujours déplacé."* He sighed heavily, then tried to cover the sigh with a chuckle.

Amy watched him dragging himself up the stairs by the bannister, while her love for him flooded back in tender pity. It had been obscured for weeks. Hidden behind the tempestuous emotions which had nearly overwhelmed her.

Amy saw Martin and Claire, arm in arm, strolling toward the bayou. *They* were happy, anyway. She wandered aimlessly along the front of the mansion until she reached another grove of live oaks, the long gray moss hanging from their branches. She thought of the legend Azilde had told them at dinner. Long ago in the days of the fierce Attakapas, lovelorn Indian maidens had hanged themselves from the live oaks. Their entangled black tresses caught on the branches, and had turned gray through the centuries. Claire had laughed and said that didn't make sense, or else there were millions of lovelorn Indian maidens since the whole deep South was covered with moss. Martin pinched her cheek and said, "Don't be so literal, darling. Anyway, around here the air must be conducive to heartbroken maidens—look at Evangeline!" Then they had both started and glanced at Amy. She was blissfully munching pecan pie, but noted their concerned glances, and was puzzled. Did they think that the mention of that make-believe girl would upset her? Did they think she wanted to see the statue at St. Martinville?—Why, she knew from her readings that there was another statue at Grand Pré in Nova Scotia, erected in honor of the same fictitious woman, and her own interest in the poem had waned months ago.

And yet, as she wandered through the live oaks, the camellia bushes, the luxuriant azaleas, dormant now in winter, a curious sense of purpose, of something she must do—gradually came over her. Like the day in Greenwich, when she had been compelled to visit the Bush-Holley House. She walked up a path toward a low white building—the garage, which had once been stables, and saw Ben relaxing in the sun, his legs up on a box, his elbow resting on the Cadillac's fender, his battered straw hat tipped over his eyes.

"G'afternoon, missy," he said, pushing up his hat when he heard her footsteps on the brick path. "Yo' explorin'?—Ol' slave quarters up yondah," he pointed to a row of white-washed cabins. "We don' use 'em fur nothin', now-a-days 'cept stores an' tools, but visitors, they gen'ally likes to see 'em."

Slave quarters, thought Amy . . . far away and long ago there had been other slave quarters . . . bondage —me too—the bond servant—but then worse and no one to help . . . pain, misery, agonizing screams from a wash house—little Candy.

Ben straightened up at the expression on the Yankee girl's face—like she heard something scary, like she was going to cry.

"No call t' look lak dat, missy," he said soothingly. "Slavery days is ovah and wasn't never no cruel mastah
159

at Bellerive, m' gran'pappy tol' me, we was *fambly,* an' proud ter be Lavals, We still is."

Amy's feeling of anguish passed. She blinked and heard Ben. She had a fleeting wonder what Jeb would think of Ben's remark, and could hear Jeb's indignant scorn, but her sense of immediate urgency grew stronger. Something pushing, teasing at her.

"Ben," she said, "did you say in the airport last night there was some Delatours hereabouts?"

"Sho' did." Ben smiled his dazzling smile. "They's mighty fine Cajuns, though lak all o' 'em they keeps purty much to theirsel's. Still, times I drive ter Ma'tinville, they often ax me in fur coffee."

"I'd like to meet them," said Amy. "D'you think I could?"

"Sho' 'nuff," answered Ben, after a thoughtful moment. He knew how his mistress felt about Cajuns, not despising them exactly, she simply didn't care to know them, but he was also certain that she would refuse no favor to a guest. "I could run yo' up ter see 'em," he said, " 'twouldn't take long." He glanced at the beloved Cadillac. No, that wouldn't do. "We'd go in the truck."

Amy nodded slowly. "I'd like to bring my grandfather, too . . . I've got to!" she added with a vehemence which surprised herself, as it did Ben. He stared at her set face, it had grown white as the garage door next to her, behind the spectacles he could see her gray eyes opened wide and fixed. She looked almost like she'd seen a ghost.

"You *got* t' take the old gennleman?" he repeated, frowning, "but ain't he sick, gone ter lie down?"

She caught her breath. "Yes, he's sick . . . Ben, I'm frightened. Something's telling me, there's a dark shadow coming near . . ."

Then Ben understood with all the primal intuition of his race. He remembered, too, that Cindy's old hound-dog had three times howled in the night. And yesterday before he set out for the airport, he had seen a black buzzard slowly circling to the *left* above the bayou. His scalp prickled, and he said gravely, "We'll take yoah gran'pappy missy, iffen yo' think 'twould do him good. I'll help you get him t' the truck."

Amy and Ben had no trouble extracting Pierre Dela-tour from the quiet mansion; he had not been able to sleep and greeted Amy's appearance with tremulous pleasure. He was quite willing to go anywhere that she wanted. He brightened considerably when he found they were to take a ride in a truck, and hardly needed Ben and Amy's help in clambering to the seat.

They rattled and banged up the road along the bay-ou for several miles. Around a bend their driver slowed down and pointed, "In here, missy," Ben said very low to Amy. He saw that her grandfather was nod-ding, half asleep against the girl, and he didn't look too good. His face kind of pinched and bloodless.

Amy stared at the mail box marked DELATOUR. Be-hind it were two large, neatly bordered vegetable patches, a barn, a chicken house with a run from which came a chorus of squawks and clucks. There were two old cars and a dilapidated buggy near the barn. Set farther back under chinaberry trees and live oaks stood a small steep-roofed gray cypress house with a very deep front porch or galérie, and a brick and mud chim-ney from which curled a wisp of blue smoke. Amy saw many figures on the galérie, and heard an accordion and a burst of singing. Ben turned up the rutted drive. There was a stir on the galérie, three children ran down the steps, followed by a burly mustachioed man in a black suit not unlike Grandpère's.

The man came toward the truck. " 'Ola, Ben!" he cried cordially. "*Pourquoi* you go to Martinville on Sunday—*hein?* You got secret rendezvous? You mak' ze horns for Cindy—yes?" He laughed uproariously, then he saw the two strangers beside Ben, and stopped laughing, his brown eyes hardened. "Who you got zere?"

Amy pushed past her grandfather and jumped off the truck, running up to the stout, middle-aged man, and holding out her hand. *"Nous sommes les Delatours —du Canada, monsieur,"* she cried. *"Moi et man grandpère—je crois qu'il est mourant!"*

Henri Delatour gaped, his wits were keen, but he could not comprehend this little girl in the touristique shameless red pants, who looked at him with a kind of anguish, who spoke perfect French, who said that she thought her grandfather was dying. He turned slowly and called toward the porch, *"Lisette! Viens ici!"*

A handsome aproned woman came down the steps, she had a baby in her arms, another child clinging to her full skirts. *"Qu'a-t-il? Qu'a-t-il?"* she said impatiently, for she had been about to serve coffee and cakes to the friends and relatives who had dropped in this Sunday afternoon. Then she looked hard at Amy, who made a mute gesture toward the truck. She peered at old Pierre.

"We are Delatours, madame!" cried Amy desperately in French. *"Please receive us!"*

Things happened fast after that. Élisette, while scolding her husband for having a donkey's brain, bustled and commanded. She got them all, including Ben, installed in her kitchen. She made old Pierre sit in the biggest armchair, the *"fauteuil,"* usually reserved for her own father. She brought him fragrant ink-black coffee from the pot on the stove. She shooed the crowding, whispering children outside. She told her guests to stay out on the galérie, while Pierre, amazed and bewildered, clung to Amy's hand. *"Qui sont-ils?"* he whispered. *"Où sommes-nous? Je ne comprend pas."*

Amy watched his color return. She looked at

162

Élisette, at Henri, now both anxiously hovering, she put her cheek against her grandfather's. "I think you are with your own at last," she whispered, "no longer *déplacé*."

That December afternoon on the Bayou Teche provided the happiest hours of Amy's life to date. She watched her grandfather revive and bloom when he understood where he was. *This* time her uncanny compulsion, her sense of other-worldly purpose and action had not ended in frustrated misery. Here, there was no abnormal frightening confusion with a time long past. For these indeed were their kin folk.

Henri Delatour sent his wife to a carved oaken chest in the *grenier* or attic, where she found the old *Contrat de Mariage* he had sent her for. It was a parchment, wrapped in oilskin, and written by a priest in 1769. The contract attested the marriage of Henri Delatour and Marie LeBlanc, but it was the paragraph of archaic French writing on the back which Henri wished to consult. Though he had never tried to read it himself, he remembered what it pertained to.

By this time the eight adults on the porch, and an assortment of children had all sifted curiously back into the big kitchen, and stood near the door, murmuring.

They were beginning to understand that this was a singular event, nothing so remarkable and unexpected had happened on the Teche since old Bo-bo Mouton's house was struck by lightning.

Amy was hardly aware of all the faces as Henri handed her the parchment, after squinting at the paragraph uncertainly. "You can read it, *non?*" he asked, instinctively knowing that she had more formal education than any of them. Amy slowly deciphered the scanty information recorded by that eighteenth-century priest, doubtless at the request of someone who saw the importance of a record.

The faded writing said that the first Henri had been one of two Delatour brothers who had finally made their way to the Louisiana bayous, nine years after *"Le Grand Dérangement"* in Acadia, then pioneered here on the Teche. The younger brother was Henri, who was married this day by the below-signed Jesuit missionary, Père Jean Cambon, and the older brother was—Paul.

"See—" interrupted Élisette proudly, "even today we have always a 'Paul' in the family . . . ! 'Ti-Paul, come here, where are you?"

A tall youth of about nineteen edged sheepishly from the crowd and approached his mother. *"Dis 'allo à Ange-Marie et son grandpère,"* commanded Élisette. "They are Delatours, also—yes!"

Paul bobbed his head. Amy raised hers and looked at him earnestly, at his curly dark hair, his gray eyes like her own, his olive-skinned square face. *"Paul,"* she thought. Why did the name bring with it a thrill of yearning, of tenderness? She did not know, but she smiled at the lad in a way that made him blush, and look at her with startled attention.

"That Paul did not remain here," said Henri. "We have a story in the family, he went back North to find his fiancée, we do not know if he did."

Grandpère suddenly leaned forward, and nodded repeatedly. *"Ouais—"* he cried. "He *did!* It was Paul who was our ancestor, Ange-Marie's and mine, now I remember the name, he went back to Acadie—then we are *related—"* added the old man to Henri, in great excitement, "I did not think I had any of my own blood left on earth!"

"Calme-toi, cheri," said Amy, stroking his hand and forcing him to lie back in the chair. She could feel his pulse pounding, she saw tears in his eyes. Now they

were all milling around the kitchen, the LeBlancs, the Broussards, and the children. They each kissed Amy and her grandfather on both cheeks. They exclaimed. Terence LeBlanc began a jubilant Cajun tune on his accordion. Someone cried that they must hold a dance to celebrate the reunion. A real *"Fais-dodo."* Someone else said what a marvel this was, Delatours from Quebec—just now when they were instigating closer ties with Quebec, when French was at last permitted in the schools, after being suppressed so long. They assumed the new-found relations had come straight from Canada, and Amy felt an unexpected pang of disloyalty. For Grandpère it was different, and she perceived that he had actually wiped out all the unhappy years in Connecticut. But I *was* born there, thought Amy, and my mother *is* Yankee. She had a dim realization that it was the first time she had ever emotionally accepted these facts, but she did not want to dampen her grandfather's joy, and kept silent.

They all drank black coffee and ate flaky cookies Élisette had prepared. *"Oreilles de Cochon,"* so-called from their pig-eared shape. Grandpère thought that very funny. There was music, the children danced around the kitchen and the other downstairs room— the parlor, which Élisette threw open for the occasion. Grandpère tapped the rhythm on the arm of his chair, he did not know the Cajun words but many of the tunes he had heard in his Canadian boyhood, and he hummed along with the others.

"Ah-ah, *'Ti*-Paul," cried Henri to his son, as he gathered up his protesting wife, "I danse with *'ma vielle'* you danse with Ange-Marie, your new cousine —yes!"

The youth came up shyly to Amy, *"Veux-tu?"* he asked. She hesitated, then laughed. "Why not?" She took off her glasses and tucked them in Grandpère's pocket. She let Paul seize her hands, and gallop her around the rooms and out on the galérie, to the strains of *"Allons à Lafayette"* and *"Danse Calinda-Boum doum-doum."*

Her cheeks grew pink, her eyes sparkled, her hair flew around her shoulders, she heard a comment, *"Elle est jolie-jolie, la 'tite Québequoise,"* and knew from his expression that Paul thought her pretty too. When Terence put down the accordion and mopped his forehead, Paul drew her outside to a corner of the galérie, asked if he could see her again, and looked dismayed when she said she was staying at Bellerive, though he continued to talk, with less assurance. He told her that he worked in a sugar plant in New Iberia, but he would, of course, have Christmas off—perhaps on Christmas Day, or the following Saturday, they might meet again . . .

Amy had no time to answer, nor knew what her answer would be, for Ben, who had stayed in the kitchen chatting in "Gumbo French" to little Lala, the youngest Delatour daughter, suddenly appeared on the galérie.

"I'm afraid yo' gran'pappy's took real bad, missy," he said, his brown face grave in the sunset light. Amy caught her breath and ran inside where they had all grown quiet. Élisette was bending over the armchair.

"Le docteur—le curé," she cried to her husband. *"Téléphone au curé—"*

But there was no time left for doctor or priest.

Amy rushed to the old man who was slumped forward, his breathing stertorous. "His pills—" she cried, and grabbed the little vial from his pocket. She forced one into his mouth. In a minute he stirred and looked at Amy. *"C'est fini—"* he whispered, gasping. *"Ne pleure pas pour moi."* He smiled for a second. *"Je suis content."* His whole body shivered and was still.

One by one all the company, including the children slowly fell to their knees on the scrubbed cypress planks, they crossed themselves, and led by Henri, they prayed in solemn unison. *"De profundis clamavi ad te —Domine—"* while a gentle wind stirred the leaves outside, and twilight fell along the Teche.

Chapter Eight

Pierre Delatour was buried the next day, Monday, December 24, at three in the afternoon, buried in the Delatour private cemetery near the banks of the Teche. Martin helped arrange the burial after Ben came back in the truck and solemnly announced to those waiting anxiously at Bellerive exactly what had happened; they had been astounded at the disappearance of Amy and her grandfather.

"Oh, the poah old gentleman," cried Azilde, her eyes readily filling with tears. "What a dreadful thing, dyin' there alone with those Cajuns, if he'd stayed here with his friends we'd have got a doctor, and he shouldn't have exerted himself like that. Oh dear, Oh dear, and Christmas so near and the weddin'."

"Those Cajuns were his kin-folk, Mother," said Martin quietly. "He died happy, Ben says so. Amy knew what she was doing when she took him there. But because of Christmas, and because there's no use in prolonging Amy's grief, the funeral should be tomorrow. I'm going to consult with Henri Delatour, I'm going there right now."

"So am I . . ." said Claire. She was stricken for Amy, afraid of what this new shock would do to the girl.

Azilde nodded reluctantly. "I suppose you should go to pay respects. They'll hold a wake, a 'Veillée,' those people always do. Amy should have a black dress, I'll find something—it nevah occurred to me that nice Mr. Delatour had *Cajun* kin-folk. Oh, this is very bad luck —a funeral just *now,* though I thank Our Blessed Lord that it's not one of the family." Her lovely face looked so worried that Martin said briskly, "Better a funeral first, and then a wedding, instead of the other way around. We'll be pretty late for dinner, darling, may have to skip it entirely."

"But you two don't have to stay that long. Cindy's makin' your favorite crab soufflé, and the special beef Bourguignon!" cried Azilde, who begrudged every minute that her son could not be with her, and was feeling resentment that the peculiar northern guests were causing so much trouble, that they had tainted Bellerive's charmed serenity with sudden death, though she was too well-bred to say so outright. Martin understood and kissed her quickly, then he and Claire hurried out to the garage.

When they reached the Delatours the curé from St. Martinville was already there, and had said the Benediction and prayers for the dead.

The best bed had been brought down from upstairs into the parlor, with its mattress of Spanish moss and chicken feathers covered by an heirloom spread of coarse white lace. Tapers were burning and votive lights before the household shrine to the Virgin. There were many people in the two rooms and out on the *galérie,* all speaking in hushed murmurs. Élisette was making coffee, while stirring bits of shrimp, chicken, sausage, tomatoes with rice in a huge iron pot, for the savory brown "Jumbalaya" to be served later at the *Veillée.* Neighbors had hurriedly brought in most of the ingredients.

Henri came to the kitchen door when he heard the blue Cadillac draw up outside. He stood defensively in the doorway, barring entrance. Hostility was plain in his stare when Martin mounted the steps to the *galérie* and introduced Claire and himself.

Henri responded with only a mutter. For why were these haughty Creoles who didn't even speak French pushing in like this? In a time of sorrow. They would take care of their own here, of the new-found cousin so quickly lost to them.

"You go back to Bellerive, yes," said Henri, standing firm in the doorway. "Leave us tranquille with our dead. You 'ave no place 'ere—*non!*" Henri made an eloquent dismissing motion with his hands. The crowd murmured agreement, though the priest stepped up and frowned uncertainly.

"We *have* a place here," cried Claire, speaking with sure instinct to Élisette who had left the stove to stand behind her husband. "We were fond of M. Delatour, and we love Amy—Ange-Marie," she amended. "See, I've brought her mourning to put on," and she held out the black dress provided by Azilde.

Élisette looked at Claire, at the black dress, and her face cleared. This gesture was proper, it showed heart. "*Vous aimez*—you love la 'tite Ange-Marie?" she asked slowly.

Claire nodded emphatically. "She is to be my bridesmaid next Thursday. Mr. Stone and I," she put her hand on Martin's arm, "are being married then at Bellerive."

As Henri still hesitated, the curé pressed forward. Though she was not of his parish, he knew all about Azilde de Laval Stone, as did everyone who lived along the Teche. "*Qu'ils entrent,*" he said to Henri sternly, and then to Claire. "Ange-Marie is sitting with her gran'father, she need consolation."

After the priest spoke, Henri gradually thawed. He talked with Martin aside in a corner of the kitchen, and it turned out that they were in complete accord on the expediency of holding the funeral tomorrow, only

170

Henri had been unsure as to how it could be done so fast. Moreover, there was the awkward question of expense. Henri had some savings—as what Frenchman did not? Still, there wasn't much. The sugar crop poor this year, the hens not laying as they should. Martin cut in crisply. "I'll take all the charges for the funeral, M. Delatour, we have an obligation to our guests at Bellerive."

Henri could not hide his relief, nor questioned further. "Obligations," he could understand. They must be honored. "You good fellow, I t'ink, *oui!*" he said at last, shaking Martin's hand. "Can you get *ze entrepreneur*—'ow you say—undertaker? 'E sometime wait many many days to come."

"I think I can," said Martin, and he went to the wall telephone he saw by a kitchen shelf.

Thus it was that Pierre Delatour was laid to rest in a country so far from his place of birth, yet among the graves of his own people, and bade farewell to in his own language.

Amy, wearing the black dress, hastily shortened and fitted by Élisette's skilled fingers, cast into the grave the first shell, thinking that Grandpère would have been amused, perhaps. In this country they did not drop clods of earth into the grave, they used shells, pretty shells brought up from the Gulf, or even scrubbed, pearly-lined soft water clams. She could notice things like that because she was not anguished. There was sadness, of course, she had wept softly last night when Claire came to her, while she sat beside the bed where Grandpère lay so waxen pale, a faint smile on his bearded lips. She had wept during the *Veillée*, but there was warmth and comfort to sustain her—all the kind French people—with them she felt at ease, Claire and Martin too, it was good to have them with her at this time. Besides, Grandpère had said, *"Ne*

171

pleure pas pour moi, je suis content." And she knew that he was happier than he had ever been on earth.

She pushed up the little black veil, lent by one of the LeBlancs, and watched the other mourners, Henri, Élisette, LeBlancs, Broussards, Moutons—unknown relations—solemnly casting their shells into the grave. At the curé's gesture, so did Claire and Martin, all saying good-by to the good old man whose body would rest forever in this peaceful cemetery beside the bayou, under the cypresses and the trailing moss.

It did not surprise Amy that Mrs. Stone had not come to the funeral, it was impossible to imagine Azilde being jostled in that hearty, noisy Cajun kitchen, drinking coffee from earthen mugs, being tripped over by the children, or subjecting herself to the boisterous highly flavored Cajun humor which broke through at intervals, and was in no way disrespectful to the dead.

Yet Martin had been annoyed at his mother's stubborn refusal to attend with Claire and himself. "O' course, honey, we must be charitable, I'll be glad to contribute any way I should—I know those folks are poor—I'll send a Christmas cake by Ben, and Cindy's sure to have table scraps left, since you didn't eat that delicious Boeuf Bourguignon last night—"

"Mother!" Martin exclaimed in a tone she had only heard once or twice from her husband, "these people don't want your table scraps—they don't want any more to do with you than you do with them, and I'm sorry I mentioned the funeral at all."

A crease appeared on Azilde's ivory forehead, she looked hurt and bewildered. "I decleah, I don't know why you're fussin' at me, spoilin' everything—those misahble Cajuns—and on Christmas Eve. . . ."

Martin heaved an exasperated sigh and gave it up.

"What did you expect?" said Claire when he told her. "And when you come down to it, she's behaved very well to *our* Delatours, whom we sprang on her

172

from the blue." They were walking back from the burial, a little apart from the mourners who were mostly dressed in black—everybody had black clothes ready-stored for funerals, if they didn't wear them regularly on Sundays for Mass.

"I wonder if Amy could have found her Paul at last!" added Claire, looking toward the head of the procession, where the girl's black figure could be seen half turned to the tall, young son of Henri and Élisette, while he bent over her protectively.

"It's a weird coincidence," said Martin, also surveying the young couple.

"Not at all," said Claire, smiling. "Perfectly natural, a line of 'Pauls' named for the first one, the brother who was lost to them forever when he went north, and not strange that she should find Delatours on the bayou, considering the Acadian history, and don't go telling me this Paul is a reincarnation of her husband Paul so long ago, because I don't believe it. Only Amy's a psychic, a 'sensitive,' that I'll allow, and we've certainly seen some strange manifestations. Gosh, darling, that awful night when she was reliving in the present, and on her own body, the horror of being burned alive." Claire shuddered. "I can't explain that one."

Nor could Martin, though his interest in para-psychology had been confirmed, and he meant to study the subject in depth next year.

"The question is," he said as they approached the Delatour *galérie* and the horde of gesticulating Cajuns, "what do we do with poor Amy *now?* Greenwich and the impossible Sarah will be ever grimmer for her without her grandfather, and there's the Mac Wilton business—how can she handle that . . . heartbreak?"

"I think," said Claire, watching Amy, who was smiling rather absently up at 'Ti-Paul, "that the girl has

173

suddenly grown up. I think she'll be able to make decisions for herself."

And so it proved. Amy went back with her good friends to Bellerive at five, and Azilde, touched by the little figure in the black dress greeted her with genuine sympathy, which Amy accepted in a composed, grateful way. She was no longer overpowered by Azilde, nor the luxury surrounding her, and after a few minutes she said, "Please, would you mind if I phoned Mother? I want to tell her."

Claire and Martin were at once contrite. Nobody had thought to notify Sarah.

"O' course, sugar," cried Azilde, "nearest phone's in the library, you can be private there."

In a few minutes Amy walked slowly back from the telephone, and joined the three others in the drawing room. She would never forget her mother's cry when she understood what had happened. "Oh, Amy child —I'm right *sorry*," there was a pause, then Sarah said in a strangled voice, "I wish I hadda been nicer to him." The tone and words were of a kind Amy had never heard from her mother, nor the tenor of what followed. "I know how bad you feel, dear, try to forget and have fun now—the wedding and all. Don't hurry back if they want you to stay. And I'm doing fine, just fine." Yet Amy had the strong impression that her mother was not well.

Amy was silent through the Christmas Eve supper, which consisted entirely of fish, as was proper on this night of penitence and fasting. She went to Midnight Mass with the others in St. Peter's Church, and thought the service beautiful. She found that she could pray, or at least feel a dreamy sense of communion with something beyond herself—something magical and comforting.

She slept well that night at Bellerive, no longer daunted by the immensity of her room, nor frightened by the bathroom mirrors. She was oblivious to them. She was awakened on Christmas morning by the snapping of firecrackers, the jubilant voices of the Negroes shouting, "Me'y Chrissmus! Me'y Chrissmus!" outside her windows.

On Christmas afternoon, Ramon lit a hundred candles on the Christmas tree—a native pine, decorated with popcorn strings and filigree glass baubles, long preserved in the Laval family. There were presents under the tree. Amy was overcome and embarrassed by hers. A large tapestry tote bag from Claire—much like the one Doris Drake carried. A dozen really good ball-point pens in a leather case initialed A.D., from Martin. A gold medal of the Virgin on a fine gold chain from Azilde, who explained that she had, of course, had it blessed by the curé at St. Peter's.

"But, I've nothing for *you!*" Amy cried, flushing. "I didn't think . . ." At home the only Christmas presents had been some trinket or box carved by Grandpère for her, and the handkerchief she always scrimped to buy for him. Otherwise, Christmas was like any holiday.

Azilde and the others laughed and soothed her discomfiture, but Amy had a perception of gracious generosity she would never forget.

Azilde kept open house, and many guests dropped in for eggnog. The old plantation families came calling from Lafayette, St. Martinville, as far away as Franklin. They were cordial to Amy, but as Amy knew none of them, nor found anything to say, they respected her bereavement, and gathered in a laughing group around the betrothed couple, Claire and Martin.

Amy slipped outside just as the Christmas fireworks began. Ben set them off in the gardens. She was dazzled, thrilled, as she watched the display from near a post on the back verandah. She had seen Fourth of July fireworks in Bruce Park at home, but none like these. Soon all the guests crowded out to watch, and Amy edged along the house until she came to the base of the great kitchen chimney. There she stood, alone, waiting for each burst of waterfalls, brilliant flower pots, and dragons, followed by showers of golden stars against the black sky. She jumped when she felt a hand on her arm, and peered up at a man's figure. " 'Ti-Paul," she whispered in amazement. The youth nodded. By the brilliance of the next firework she could see him looking down at her with anxiety, tenderness. He explained in his rapid patois that he had wanted so much to see her, his mother had teased him and said it was *"le coup de foudre,"* the lightning bolt of love at first sight, but they had let him take the family car.

He had walked around and around Bellerive, hoping to catch a glimpse of her, and now he had found her so fortunately alone. He waited until the booms of the new set-piece were over, then said, *"Je suis sérieux, Ange-Marie—tu comprends—oui?"*

She bowed her head, ignoring the next fairy shower of golden stars dropping into the Teche. Yes, she believed him, that he was serious, she knew that he meant marriage, and she was deeply touched.

"I'm too young," she murmured, "it's too soon. I like you, 'Ti-Paul, very much, but you don't know me, I'm only half Delatour, you do not know the way I really live . . ."

He swept his arm out in a gesture which encircled the whole of the plantation, the elegantly dressed guests on the verandah—"You live like *this?*" he asked sadly.

"Oh no," she laughed with a catch in her breath. "Not like *this.*"

"I'll wait," he said. "When you go up there *dans ce pays étrange,* will you write to me? Let me know when you're coming back?"

"I'll write," she said, "and I *shall* be back somehow, someday, if only to put flowers on Grandpère's grave."

He sighed, his body drooped. He took her hand, gave it a clumsy kiss, and disappeared into the shadows of the live oaks.

Amy skipped the last firework, an American flag in full color, and walked slowly upstairs to her room. She sat down in one of the rose velvet armchairs and began to think. She sat there half an hour trying to straighten out her feelings, trying to realize that she had just received her first proposal, feeling warm gratitude to 'Ti-Paul. He and his family were dear to her, and yet—

There was an impatient tap on her door, and Shirley, the black chambermaid, bounced in.

"You is the disappearin'est girl," she said pertly. "We'se been lookin' all ovah fo' you. Dinnah's waitin', 'sides, there was a telephone call fo' you from up No'th —Connetchicut—some outlandish name."

"Connecticut?" repeated Amy, her eyes widening. "Oh, not *mother!*"

Shirley saw the sudden fear, and inspecting the black dress, spoke with less disapproval. "Dunno, Ramon, he tuk the call, ever'body was watchin' fireworks. Ramon say the party'll call back in an hour."

Amy got up slowly, pushing her hair off her shoulders. Mother wouldn't use the phone again unless something had happened. Oh, dear Lord . . .

Shirley watched her critically. "Got yo' bridesmaid dress 'most ready, size ten, lak Ol' Missy say, jest need final fittin'. I can sew real good. D'you think I c'ld get me a job up No'th?"

"I don't *know*, Shirley," said Amy, hurrying past the black girl who looked peevish. "I've got to get near that phone."

The phone rang as Amy reached the great hall. Martin answered it, and came out of the library. When he saw Amy he said, "Long distance for you."

"What is it?" she whispered, moistening her lips.

"I've no idea, Amy, I only talked to the operator. We'll be right in the next room, my dear, if you need us."

Amy picked up the receiver and said, "Hello," faintly; she gave her name to the operator, and waited.

"Amy? That you at last?" said an eager male voice.

Amy stared at the phone, "Mac—" she breathed incredulously.

"What? I can't hear you, is this Amy Delayter?"

She cleared her throat and swallowed. "Yes—it's me. I—I thought you were skiing . . ."

"I was . . . snow's lousy. I came home. As a matter of fact, the company was lousy, too. I sort of missed you, Amy. I thought I'd wish you Merry Christmas."

"Same to you," she said, her voice now under control. "Mac . . . Grandfather died. He was buried yesterday."

There was a startled pause, then Mac said, "Gee, I'm sorry, awful sorry, I know how you felt about him. Gee, that's terrible for you."

"No," said Amy, "I'm glad that he died happy. Glad he died like he did."

There was another pause, before Mac spoke again. "I suppose after this . . . you won't want to do what I was going to ask . . ."

"What did you want me to do, Mac?"

"There's a dance, Saturday night at a restaurant. We've hired the whole restaurant. A whole bunch of the kids are going. I thought maybe you'd be my date?"

Again, Amy stared at the receiver. How desperately excited this invitation would have made her a week ago, she would have been shattered, weeping with joy and trying to hide it. Now, she merely felt a pleasant glow, tinged with vast relief that the phone carried no bad news from her mother.

"I'd like to go, Mac," she said quietly. "You know I

don't dance very well." She thought of the exuberant dancing she had done with 'Ti-Paul, just before Grand-père died.

"Aw . . . I could teach you enough in ten minutes," said Mac. "Amy, are you coming back in time? Will you be my date?"

"Yes," she said, "thanks for asking me. You know, Mac, I thought you didn't like me, after that—that evening at your house—I'm not quite sure what happened—"

"Forget it!" answered the voice roughly. "Everything was all screwed up that night. I've been doing some thinking. It's funny, I can't keep you out of my mind. I honestly don't understand it, but I've got to tell it like it is. Good-by for now, I'll be seeing you *soon?*"

"Yes," said Amy, and hung up. She walked into the drawing room where her elders were waiting.

"That was Mac Wilton," she said to Martin. "He asked me to a dance on Saturday night, I said I'd go."

Martin and Claire gaped at her. The casual announcement, the calm little face in contrast to the girl's devastation, her hysteria, of three days ago, and many weeks before that. Though Claire had expected a new maturity, this change was so total that Claire barely suppressed a nervous laugh.

"But, honey—you cain't go home so soon!" protested Azilde, the crease appearing on her brow. "That's hardly a visit at all, I thought you'd stay through New Year's with me. I'm goin' to be mighty lonesome when these two leave for their honeymoon. O' course, there'll be a few left over from the weddin'—the de la Falaisses, the Claibornes from N'Yawlins—they're quite young, you'd have fun with them, and I'd *like* to have you."

Azilde spoke sincerely. Quite aside from her hospitable instincts, she was developing a fondness for the

179

girl. There was pathos in that little black-robed figure, in mourning like herself, and so much could be done to bring out the girl's charm, like having a daughter to mold, to instill with the graces of a true southern gentlewoman, despite that unfortunate Cajun connection . . . which could be ignored. "You'll stay on, Amy," she said with the gentle authority which nobody ever disobeyed, except Martin.

"I can't, Mrs. Stone," said Amy flatly. "It's sweet of you to ask me, and I'll come back sometime, if you'll have me, but my mother's not too well, she needs me —and besides . . ." She paused, twisting her hands in the old way, and Martin spoke rather sharply.

"Besides, you wouldn't miss the date with Mac for anything?" He now saw how Mac had got Amy's address in the glass corridor that last day of school, and he feared Amy's reinvolvement with the boy. It had led to nothing but trouble before.

"It's not Mac—" said Amy, taken aback by the sharpness. "I'll be glad to go to the dance with him, it'll be nice. We can start over, he said, so." She frowned, looking at Claire. "It's funny, I can't remember *why* I was so upset over Mac. I know I was. I acted pretty crazy, didn't I?"

Claire looked back at the girl with affection and amusement. "You did, sort of—" she said temperately. "And there were reasons we won't go into." Will *never* go into, she added to herself. Amy had left all the turmoil of her identification with the other Ange-Marie behind. She had crossed the dividing line back to sanity. Claire knew this by intuition and by experience, yet there was one more question.

"Your mother doesn't expect you so soon, dear, and you say the date with Mac isn't all *that* important, then why don't you stay on here a bit at Bellerive. Mrs. Stone really wants you."

"Why, there's my *work*," said the girl, as though the

answer were obvious. "My grades fell off terribly last term, didn't they?" She looked at Martin, who was astonished and nodded slowly.

"I've got to catch up," said Amy, "get back early and find the assignments, do a lot of reading . . . I mean to take the S.A.T. and College Boards, as soon as I can qualify."

"Jeepers . . ." whistled Martin, on a long breath. His wondering eyes met Claire's. She smiled and shrugged.

Azilde, to whom Amy's remark was gibberish, looked perplexed though she had grasped one factor which she could understand. Was this "Mac" the boy who had crossed Amy in love? If he'd come around and was telephoning her, that would be a reason for the determination to go North, though the girl didn't seem exactly thrilled.

"And another thing," said Amy earnestly, "Mr. Stone, I'm afraid I'll never be able to finish Longfellow for independent studies. Next term I'd like to do something you suggested once, I think you did."

"What?" said Martin, gradually recovering from his amazement.

"The French-speaking peoples of North America. I believe I could manage that."

Martin swallowed. "There's no student in the Greenwich High School better qualified . . ." he said gravely, then he burst out laughing. "Go to it, Amy! You've got what it takes, kid. You're making Claire and me very happy. I'll switch your plane reservation for you tomorrow. The twenty-eighth do? You *can't* leave before the wedding, you know, even with this newfound zeal for work!"

"I wouldn't want to." Amy smiled the sudden dimpled smile which transfigured her. "You and Claire are my best friends in the whole wide world."

On December twenty-eighth, Amy sat alone on the Delta plane bound nonstop for Kennedy Airport. She knew exactly what to do, had instructions in the tapestry tote bag Claire had given her for Christmas. The instructions were simple. At Kennedy, ask for the Connecticut Limousine, take it and get off in Greenwich at the Show Boat Motor Inn. From there she could walk to her flat over the deli, though her canvas suitcase was a lot heavier than when she left. Besides the other gifts, it contained the bridesmaid dress, a lovely creation of turquoise chiffon edged around the neck and on the sleeves with velvet ribbon. There was a turquoise velvet belt, too. At the ceremony she had carried a stiff bouquet of pink camellias, and worn a little cap of camellias on her head, pinned to the glossy chestnut hair which fell nearly to her waist. She had faced the mirrors in her magnificent bathroom with pleasure. She knew that she looked pretty, and had then forgotten herself in admiration of the bride and groom. Claire, so radiant in ivory satin, Martin so dignified in a frock coat with pearl-gray pants. She remembered their long kiss in the rectory parlor, after the priest said, "I pronounce you man and wife," and the beautiful solemn way they looked deep into each other's eyes. It sent shivers down her back. Later at Bellerive for the reception, events had blurred. There was such a bustle of caterers from New Iberia, so much scent of flowers and perfume mingled and the insistent strains of the four-piece orchestra Azilde had hired, so much unknown food, and champagne which prickled her nose, and so many strangers—only fifty, Azilde sadly said earlier, when they could have had three hundred, except for Martin and Claire's insistence on a small wedding.

Well, so much of everything that Amy could no longer recapture details, except at the end, when the newlyweds departed in a shower of rice and confetti for the airport. Claire had remembered to kiss her, saying, "Good luck, darling, we'll be back on Steamboat Road in ten days, be seeing you then."

The new Martin Stones were going to finish the school year in Martin's apartment, while Claire commuted to New York for her own classes.

That was a happy thought, and offset a sad one. Her last plane ride . . . *Saturday?* It seemed months ago Grandpère had been next to her, leaning over to peer out the window. She could hear his eager old voice exclaiming, *"Magnifique . . . Incroyable,"* and she hadn't bothered to look at what he meant. She looked now, at the drifting cloud banks far below, beneath them glimpses of green, of red earth, while the plane itself throbbed through the blue sunshiny void. She looked to see if the other passengers were sharing her sudden exhilaration, but they all had their noses buried in newspapers or magazines, or drinks.

Amy sighed a little, and opening her tote bag drew out a small white box. Inside there was a brooch, heart-shaped, made of pearls. The sort of brooch you could buy in Woolworth's, though she had never had the money to spend on jewelry. There was a small card in the box, it said only, *"N'oublie pas—'Ti-Paul."*

This gift had made her eyes sting when Ben gave it to her in the Cadillac on the way to the airport. "Dat young Delatour brung it to me hisself this morning, he jest say give it to you, after you go." Ben chuckled, "Looks lak you made a conquest, missy."

In the plane Amy held the box with the brooch in her hand for a long time. No, she would not forget 'Ti-Paul. She would write to him. Someday she would see him again. And she knew that his sudden, inarticulate love had released her from a long, scarcely conscious misery. The name Paul, it still gave her a strange sensation, like the memory of the songs her father used to sing to her. Far off and long ago, sweetly poignant.

'Ti-Paul loved her enough to marry her. No, Amy thought, putting the little box back in her bag. I'll wait like Claire, wait years if I must, until I can give to a man, and receive from him, the look those two exchanged in the rectory parlor.

Was there once another different Paul? The question struck through her mind and seemed to pierce her heart like a shaft of blinding light. For *that* Paul had felt the way Claire felt for Martin?

The certainty that she had, passed as quickly as it came. She knew now that there was threat in such questions. Danger in any return to all the sensations which used to come when she was "dreaming true."

That was finished.

She started as she heard the pilot's voice over the loudspeaker. They were circling Kennedy, they expected to land in ten minutes. Please fasten your seat belts.

The plane dropped down through the cloud bank, everything turned gray outside the windows; they bumped onto the runway, and saw the soft whirlings of new snow. "Oh hell! Will you look at that?" said a disgusted voice behind Amy. "I wish we'd never left Louisiana!"

Amy did not agree, she loved snow and came from generations who had survived in the cold Northlands. She lifted her face to the snow as she descended the stairs from the plane. It was good to be home. A feeling of contentment which grew stronger on the limousine ride to Connecticut, and was transmuted into wonder when she saw a thin shabby figure emerge from the Show Boat Motor Inn in Greenwich. "Mother," Amy cried, flying through the snow flakes to embrace her. "Oh, I never expected you. You shouldn't have come out in this weather!"

Sarah submitted for a moment to the embrace, she even returned it, before she stiffened. "Land's sake, child, you needn't smother me. That aereoplane late? Mr. Stone said you'd be here earlier. I admit I fretted some, been waiting 'most an hour."

Amy laughed and hugged her mother again, understanding her as she never had before. "Well, I'm here now," she said, "and glad of it." She picked up her bag where it had been dumped on the sidewalk. They began to trudge together up the hill on Greenwich Avenue toward the deli.

"I do feel real bad to see you come home without Mr. Delayter," said Sarah in a muffled voice. "Just want to say that once and no more. 'Tisn't any good harking back—I've moved your things into his room, make more space for you."

They were both silent as they waited for the light to turn on Railroad Avenue. When they reached the other sidewalk, Sarah spoke again. "He left something for you, Amy, Mr. Delayter did, there was 'most three hundred dollars under his mattress, in an envelope with your name. 'Twasn't there when I turned his room out last—he—he must've had a hunch."

Amy made a sound in her throat. Though the snow had almost stopped, the few flakes drifting down misted and shimmered before Amy's eyes. "Grand-père . . ." she whispered.

Sarah talked on hastily, the worried complaining note back in her voice. "It's some help, to be sure, but I don't know what we're going to do without the mite he used to earn, when he did—though I guess there'll be something from Social Security, I don't know how long as I can support . . ."

"Mother," interrupted Amy firmly, "I'm going to get me an afternoon job. And that's that."

The decision in her daughter's voice almost quelled Sarah's automatic objections, though she said, "How'll you manage *that,* with your schoolwork? I hope you *do* some work this term."

185

"I shall," said Amy. "And, I'll manage the job. Other girls do, and I'm strong as a horse."

Sarah was silent until they had almost reached their own staircase next to the delicatessen, then she said with hesitation, "That Mac Wilton's been pestering me on the phone. Wanted to know exactly when you'd get here. I didn't tell him, didn't know as you'd want me to."

She peered hard at her daughter's face which was illumined by the street light, wondering how the child would take that, remembering all the strange things Amy had done, the frenzies, and the mooniness, the way she used to seem not really there—and that woman doctor—Mrs. Stone she must be now—had as much as admitted Mac Wilton had jilted Amy.

"Oh, I'll give Mac a call tomorrow," said the girl, resting the suitcase on the bottom step a moment. She looked around at her mother. "Mac's a great guy, I like him, of course—but there's no hurry."

"You seem different, Amy," said Sarah slowly, still examining her daughter's calm slightly smiling face. "Very different from when you left. You've changed somehow."

Amy picked up the heavy suitcase, preparatory to climbing the stairs. "I guess I am different, Mother," she said quietly, "I *have* changed—a lot."

About the Author

Anya Seton is the daughter of the famed British author-artist and naturalist, Ernest Thompson Seton. She was born in the United States as a British subject and grew up in Old and New England. Christened Ann, at five she was given the Indian name of Anutika by a Sioux Indian chief who was visiting the family, and in time, the name was shortened to Anya.

After writing and selling a number of short stories, Miss Seton began researching and writing her novels which, she says, she loves the more because the research inevitably requires travel.

The author of nearly a dozen books, several of them biographical and all of them best sellers, as well as two books for young adults, Miss Seton has made her home for many years in Greenwich, Connecticut, the setting of *Smouldering Fires*.

More Big Bestsellers from SIGNET